THE WAGGING TONGUE

Summer Edition

All the news you *have* to know!

You know it's summer in the Hamptons when the powerful and privileged let down their hair. And nowhere are the scandals flowing more freely than out at Seven Oaks Farm, playground of the Bridgehampton Polo Club.

We've all seen the beautiful movie star **Carmen Akins** cheering at the polo matches. Seems it didn't take her long to get over her divorce from her infamous director/producer husband. But it may be taking *him* a while to deal with their separation. We doubt he traveled all the way from L.A. just to view some swinging mallets. Alert the paparazzi that a silver-screen reunion may be taking place!

As far as *unions* go, haven't we all wondered if that sexy sheikh and his bashful bride are truly in a love match? **Adham** does find the best polo ponies for his clients, but has he forsaken his wife for his job? Well, you'll just have to stay for the summer to see what's in store for these couples.

BRENDA JACKSON

is a die "heart" romantic who married her childhood sweetheart and still proudly wears the "going steady" ring he gave her when she was fifteen. Because she's always believed in the power of love, Brenda's stories always have happy endings. In her real-life love story, Brenda and her husband of thirty-eight years live in Jacksonville, Florida, and have two sons.

A *New York Times* and *USA TODAY* bestselling author of more than seventy-five romance titles, Brenda is a recent retiree who now divides her time between family, writing and traveling with Gerald. You may write Brenda at P.O. Box 28267, Jacksonville, Florida 32226, by e-mail at WriterBJackson@aol.com or visit her Web site at www.brendajackson.net.

OLIVIA GATES

has always pursued creative passions—painting, singing and many handicrafts. She still does, but only one of her passions grew gratifying enough, consuming enough, to become an ongoing career. Writing.

She is most fulfilled when she is creating worlds and conflicts for her characters then exploring and untangling them bit by bit, sharing her protagonists' every heart-wrenching heartache and hope, their every heart-pounding doubt and trial, until she leads them to an indisputably earned and gloriously satisfying happy ending.

When she's not writing, she is a doctor, a wife to her own alpha male and a mother to one brilliant girl and one demanding Angora cat. Visit Olivia at www.oliviagates.com.

BRENDA JACKSON
& OLIVIA GATES

IN TOO DEEP

Published by Silhouette Books
America's Publisher of Contemporary Romance

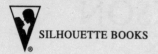 **SILHOUETTE BOOKS**

Recycling programs for this product may not exist in your area.

ISBN-13: 978-0-373-73038-4

IN TOO DEEP

Copyright © 2010 by Harlequin Books S.A.

The publisher acknowledges the copyright holders of the individual works as follows:

HUSBAND MATERIAL
Copyright © 2010 by Harlequin Books S.A.
Brenda Jackson is acknowledged as the author of "Husband Material."

THE SHEIKH'S BARGAINED BRIDE
Copyright © 2010 by Harlequin Books S.A.
Olivia Gates is acknowledged as the author of "The Sheikh's Bargained Bride."

This edition published by arrangement with Harlequin Books S.A.

For questions and comments about the quality of this book please contact us at Customer_eCare@Harlequin.ca.

® and TM are trademarks of Harlequin Books S.A., used under license. Trademarks indicated with ® are registered in the United States Patent and Trademark Office, the Canadian Trade Marks Office and in other countries.

Visit Silhouette Books at www.eHarlequin.com

Printed in U.S.A.

CONTENTS

Dear Reader,

There's nothing like a warm summer night to spark high-stakes romance! From June through August 2010, Silhouette Desire is running a new continuity miniseries—six romance-packed stories in three volumes. Escape with us to the glamorous celebrity playground of the Hamptons in A SUMMER FOR SCANDAL.

This month, *New York Times* and *USA TODAY* bestselling author Brenda Jackson teams up with Olivia Gates for the second installment: *In Too Deep* (#2025).

And *USA TODAY* bestselling author Catherine Mann joins Emily McKay to end the miniseries with *Winning It All* (#2031) in August.

These romances are the perfect summer getaway—powerful, passionate and provocative!

Happy Reading!

Krista Stroever
Senior Editor

HUSBAND MATERIAL

BRENDA JACKSON

To the love of my life, Gerald Jackson, Sr.
Happy 38th Anniversary!

She is more precious than rubies: and all the things
thou canst desire are not to be compared to her.
—Proverbs 3:15

One

Carmen Akins made her way around the huge white tent, smiling at those she recognized as neighbors, knowing most had heard about the demise of her marriage. And to make matters worse, she figured the article in last week's tabloid had probably fueled their curiosity about the man rumored to be her current lover.

They would definitely be disappointed to know her alleged affair with Bruno Casey was nothing more than a publicity stunt cooked up by their agents. Her divorce from renowned Hollywood producer and director Matthew Birmingham had made headlines, especially since they had been thought of as one of Hollywood's happiest couples. Many had followed their storybook courtship, wedding and subsequent marriage, and all had been convinced it was the perfect romance. It had come as a shock when it had all ended after three years.

Carmen had hoped she and Matthew could separate

both peacefully and quietly, but thanks to the media that had not been the case. Rumors began flying, many put into bold print in various tabloids: Oscar-winning Actress Leaves Husband for Another Man, which was followed by Renowned Producer Dumps Oscar-winning Wife for His Mistress.

Those had been two of the most widespread, although neither was true. Yes, she had been the one who'd filed for a divorce but there was no "other man" involved. And the only mistress her ex-husband had ever had while they'd been married was his work.

The first year of their marriage was everything she'd ever dreamed about. They were madly in love and couldn't stand to spend a single minute away from each other. But that second year, things began to change. Matthew's career took precedence over their relationship. She had tried talking to him but had no luck. And to keep their marriage solid, she had even turned down a couple of major movies to spend time with him. But it was no use.

The breaking point had come after she'd shot the movie *Honor.* Although Matthew had flown to France a few times to see her while she was filming, she'd wanted more private time with him without being interrupted by others on the set.

After filming had ended, she had arranged their schedules so they could spend time together in Barcelona at a secluded villa. It was there that she had planned to share with him the news that he was to become a father. She had been so happy about it—she couldn't wait for him to arrive.

But he never did.

Instead he'd called to let her know something had come up, something of vital importance, and suggested that she arrange another excursion for them at a later date. That same night, she began having severe stomach pains and heavy bleeding, and she lost their baby, a baby who, to this day, Matthew knew nothing about. Nor did he know about the time she had spent at the villa under the care of a private doctor and nurse. It was a blessing none of it had gotten to the media. The only thing Matthew knew about was the divorce papers he'd gotten a few weeks later.

She glanced around as she kept moving, not bothering to stop and strike up a conversation with anyone. There was a crowd but luckily the media was being kept off the grounds so as not to harass any celebrities in attendance. She appreciated that. It was certainly comforting since a slew of cameras had been following her around lately, especially after the rumor about Bruno had been leaked.

Her plans were to spend the entire summer in the Hamptons, watching the Bridgehampton Club polo matches at the Seven Oaks Farm. She needed some unwind time. However, she had to be careful—there were gossips everywhere and the Hamptons were no exception, especially since Ardella Rowe had purchased a home in the area. The woman was considered Joan Rivers's twin when it came to having loose lips. The secrets of more than a few celebrities who owned summer homes here had made it to the media thanks to Ardella.

"Carmen, darling."

Carmen inwardly cringed. It was as if her thoughts had conjured up the woman. She considered not answering, but several had heard Ardella call out to her and it would be rude not to respond. And while Ardella was someone you wouldn't want as a friend, you definitely wouldn't want her as an enemy, either.

Taking a deep breath, she pasted a smile on her face and turned around. The woman was right there, as if she had no intention of letting Carmen get away. Evidently she figured Carmen had some juicy news to share.

"Ardella, you're looking well," Carmen said.

"Carmen, darling, forget about me. How are *you?*" Ardella asked with fake concern, leaning over and giving her a quick kiss on her cheek. "I heard about all those horrid things Matthew Birmingham is doing to you."

Carmen lifted a brow. She could only imagine the lies being spread now. The truth of the matter was that her ex-husband wasn't doing anything to her. In fact, as far as Matthew was concerned, it was as if she had never existed. She hadn't heard from him since the day their divorce had become final a year ago. However, she had seen him in March at the Academy Awards. Like her, he'd come alone, but that had just fueled the media frenzy as they walked down the red carpet separately.

When she'd accepted her best-supporting-actress Oscar for the blockbuster hit *Honor,* it had been natural to thank him for the support and encouragement he'd given her during shooting. The media had had a field day with her speech, sparking rumors of a reconciliation between them. He had refused to comment and so had she—there was no point when both of them knew there would not be a reconciliation of any kind. Their marriage was over and they were trying to move on, namely in different directions.

Moving on had taken her a little longer than Matthew. He hadn't wasted time after their divorce was final. Seeing those photos with him and his flavor of the month had hurt, but she hadn't gotten involved with anyone to get back at him. Instead, she'd concentrated on keeping her career on top.

With a practiced smile, she said, "Why, Ardella, sweetie, you must be mistaken. Matthew isn't doing anything to me.

In fact, regardless of what you've heard, we've decided to remain friends," she proclaimed, lying through her teeth.

Matthew couldn't stand the ground she walked on. She'd heard from mutual friends that he'd said he would never forgive her for leaving him. Well, she had news for him. She would never forgive him for not being there when she'd needed him most.

"So you can't believe everything you read in those tabloids," Carmen added.

The woman gave her a shrewd look while sipping her wine. "What is this I'm hearing about you and Bruno? And I understand Matthew is seeing that lingerie model, Candy Sumlar."

Blood rushed to Carmen's head at the mention of the woman's name, but she managed to keep her cool. "Like I said, you can't believe everything you hear or read."

Ardella sharpened her gaze. "And what about what I've seen with my own eyes, Carmen? I was in L.A. a few weeks ago and I saw Matthew at a party with Candy. How do you explain that?"

Carmen gave a dignified laugh. "I don't have to explain it. Matthew and I have been divorced now for a year. He has his life and I have mine."

"But the two of you have remained friends?"

If they weren't friends this woman would be the last to know, Carmen thought, remembering the column that had appeared about her a few years back, claiming the only reason Matthew had cast her in one of his movies when she'd first started out was because they'd slept together. Sources had revealed Ardella as the person who'd spread that lie.

Thinking that one lie deserved another, Carmen acknowledged, "Yes, Matthew and I are friends. It will take more than a divorce to make us enemies." She hoped the woman never got the chance to question Matthew regarding his feelings on the matter.

Ardella gazed over Carmen's shoulder and smiled. Carmen could only hope the woman had spotted her next victim. "Well, look who's here," Ardella said, glancing back at her with a full grin on her face.

The hair on the back of Carmen's neck stood up as the tent went silent. Everyone was staring at her. Her body had begun tingling. That could only mean…

She pulled in a deep breath, hoping she was wrong but knowing from the smirk on Ardella's face that she wasn't. Matthew had entered the tent. Ardella confirmed her guess when she commented, "Looks like your ex just showed up. Imagine that. Both of you here in the Hamptons. But then, you did say the two of you *are* friends."

Carmen could tell from Ardella's tone that she was mocking Carmen's earlier claim. And from the way the tent had gotten quiet, it was clear that the spectators who'd come to see the polo game were finding the drama unfolding under the tent more interesting than what was on the field.

"He's spotted you and is headed this way. I think this is where I say farewell and skedaddle," Ardella said with a wide grin on her face.

The woman's words had Carmen wanting to run, but she stood her ground and made a quick decision. She had to believe that the man she once loved and whom she believed had once loved her would not do anything to embarrass her. She and Matthew would be civil to each other, even if it killed them. And then she would find out just why he was here. He owned the Hampton compound, but the divorce settlement gave her the right to stay there whenever she liked, as long as he remained in L.A. So why wasn't he in California? He seldom found time to come to New York.

"Carmen."

She felt his heat at the same moment she heard her name issue from his lips. Both affected her greatly. He was standing directly behind her and as much as Carmen didn't want to, she slowly turned around and feasted her gaze on her ex-husband.

Feasting was definitely the right word to use. No matter when or where she saw him, he looked as enticing as any man could. Dressed casually in a pair of tan slacks and a designer navy blue polo shirt, he was the epitome of success. And with a clean shaven head, skin the color of rich cocoa, a strong jaw line, dark piercing eyes and full lips, he had stopped more than one woman in her tracks.

Before branching out to become a director and producer, he had starred in a few movies. And when he'd been an actor, Matthew Birmingham had been considered a heart-throb. To many he still was.

Knowing they were the center of attention, she knew what she had to do, and so she did. "Matthew," she said, rising on tiptoe to plant a kiss on his cheek. "It's good seeing you."

"Same here, sweetheart."

From the tone of his voice she knew her kiss had caught him off guard, and now he was only playing along for her benefit. She felt anger beginning to boil within her at seeing him here, on her turf. This was a place he knew she enjoyed coming during the summer months, a place he conveniently stayed away from since work usually kept him on the west coast.

"I'm sure we can do better than that," he whispered.

He reached out and pulled her into his arms, claiming her mouth. His tongue slid between her parted lips and immediately began a thorough exploration. She heard the click of a cell-phone camera and figured Ardella was at work. Carmen was tempted to pull her mouth away and break off the kiss but she didn't have the willpower to do so.

It was Matthew who finally retreated, leaving her in a daze, unable to think clearly. When she saw they'd caused a scene and people were staring, she figured she had to do something before things got out of hand.

"We need to talk privately," she stated, hearing the tremble in her voice and trying to ignore the sensations in her stomach. She moved to leave the tent. As expected, he fell in step beside her.

As soon as they were away from prying eyes and extended ears, she turned to him. The smile she'd fabricated earlier was wiped clean from her face. "Why did you kiss me like that?"

He smiled and a dimple appeared in his cheek, causing a swell of longing to flow through her entire body. "Because I wanted to. And need I remind you that you kissed me first," he said in an arrogant tone.

"That was my way of saying hello."

He chuckled. "And the way I kissed you was mine."

She pulled in an irritated breath. He was being difficult and she had no time for it—or for him. "What are you doing here, Matthew? You heard the judge. I get to come here and stay—"

"As long as I remain in California," he interrupted. "Well, I'm embarking on a new business venture in New York. It was finalized today. That means I'll be relocating here for a while." His smile widened as he added, "Which means you and I are going to be housemates."

Matthew was tempted to kiss that shocked frown right off his ex-wife's face. Just knowing his words had agitated the hell out of her was the satisfaction he needed. If looks could kill, he would be a dead man.

Trying to ignore the tumultuous emotions that always overtook him whenever he saw her, he added, "Of course, you can always pack up and leave. I would certainly understand."

He knew for certain that that suggestion would rattle her even more. He was well aware of just how much she enjoyed coming here every summer to hit the beach and hang out at the polo matches. That was one of the reasons he'd purchased the compound in the first place. And if she assumed for one minute that he would allow her to sleep with her lover under the roof of a house he'd paid for, then she had another thing coming.

"How dare you, Matthew."

He couldn't help but smile at that. There was a time she had loved his outrageous dares—especially the ones he'd carried out in the bedroom. "Careful, Carmen, people are still watching. You might want to continue to play the role you created for Ardella Rowe moments ago. I rather liked it."

She looked up at him with what everyone else assumed was a warm, friendly smile, but he could see the bared teeth. His gaze flicked over her features. She was still the most beautiful woman to walk the face of the earth. He'd come into contact with numerous glamorous women, but he'd known the first time he had set eyes on Carmen five years ago, when she'd read for a part in one of his movies, that her looks would stop men dead in their tracks. And on camera or off, she gave new meaning to the word *radiant*.

"We need to talk, Matthew."

He looked away, well aware that his demeanor was distant. She had wrapped him around her finger once but she wouldn't be doing it again. He would be the first to admit he was still having problems with the fact that she'd walked out on their marriage. That said, he was only human, and if he continued to look into the depths of her dark eyes, he would remember things he didn't want to. Like how her eyes would darken when her body exploded beneath him in a climax.

He pulled in a deep breath and met her gaze again when he felt his heart harden. "No, we don't need to talk, Carmen. When you left me, you said it all. Now if you will excuse me, the first match is about to begin."

And he walked off and left her standing there.

Two

Every nerve in Carmen's body tingled in anger as she drove off the grounds of the Seven Oaks Farm. After Matthew's kiss, no doubt rumors of a possible reconciliation would begin circulating again. Feigning a headache to several people, she had gotten into her car and left.

It was a beautiful July day and as she drove past the stables in her convertible sports car, she doubted if Matthew even cared that he'd ruined what would have been a perfect afternoon for her. He'd probably known when he'd shown up what would happen, which only proved once again what a selfish person he was.

Somehow he had lost sight of what she'd told him about her parents' marriage—how her father's need to be a successful financial adviser and her mother's drive to become the most prominent real-estate agent in Memphis had isolated them from each other, which eventually led to their divorce. She had wanted more from her marriage to Matthew, but in the end, he had somehow given her even less.

Glancing around, she admired the countryside and regretted she would have to leave though she'd just gotten here yesterday. Her summer vacation had been spoiled. She pulled in a frustrated breath, wondering just what kind of business deal he'd made that would take him from California. As her hair blew in the wind she decided she really didn't care. What he did was no concern of hers.

Moments later she turned down the narrow street that led to their estate and within seconds, the sprawling beachfront home loomed before her. She could remember the first time Matthew had brought her here, months after they'd married, promising this would be the place where they would spend all of their summers. She had come every summer after that, but he'd been too busy to get away. His work had taken precedence over spending time together.

As she parked in the driveway and got out of the car, she couldn't help wondering if Matthew had plans to bring Candy Sumlar here. Would he spend more time with his girlfriend than he had his wife?

The thought that he probably would annoyed the hell out of her. She fumed all the way to the front door and slammed it shut behind her before glancing around. When she'd walked through the doors yesterday evening upon arriving, she had felt warm and welcomed. Now she felt cold and unwanted.

She quickly went upstairs, determined to pack and be miles away by the time the polo match was over and Matthew returned. There was no way he would do the gentlemanly thing and go somewhere else. It didn't matter one iota that she had been here first.

Entering the bedroom, she stopped. He had placed his luggage in here, open, on the bed. Had he been surprised to find she was already in residence? He'd wasted no time finding her to let her know he was here. And he had kissed her, of all things. She placed her fingers on her mouth, still able to feel the impression of his lips there.

Shaking off the feeling, she went to the closet and flung it open. She sucked in a deep breath. His clothes were already hanging in there, right next to hers. Seeing their clothes together reminded her of how things used to be, and her heart felt heavy and threatened to break all over again.

She pushed his clothing out the way and grabbed an armful of hers, tossing it on the bed. She was glancing around for her luggage when she suddenly felt stupid for letting Matthew ruin the summer she had been looking forward to for months. Why should she be the one to leave?

She was tired of running. For a full year following her divorce, she had avoided going to places where she thought he would be, and had stayed out of the limelight as much as she could. She had practically become a workaholic just like him, and now she wanted to have some fun. Why was she allowing him to rain on her parade, to make her life miserable when really she should be making *his* miserable?

Suddenly, she knew just the way to do it.

She hung her clothes back in the closet. It was time to give Matthew Birmingham a taste of his own medicine, Carmen style. She would work him over, do everything in her power to make it impossible for him to resist her, and then when he thought he had her just where he wanted—on her back, beneath him in bed—she would call it a wrap and leave him high and dry…and hopefully hard as a rock.

She smiled. The taste of revenge had never been sweeter.

* * *

Matthew walked into the house, closed the door behind him and glanced around. He'd been surprised to see Carmen's car parked in the driveway. He'd expected her to be long gone by now.

Ardella Rowe had sought him out during divot stomping to let him know of Carmen's headache. Of course, to keep his ex-wife's charade going he'd had to show his concern and leave immediately, though he knew she had used the headache as an excuse to slip away.

He heard her moving around upstairs and from the sounds of things she was packing. Now that she knew he was here, she wasn't wasting any time hightailing it back to wherever she'd been hiding the last few months. She was good at disappearing when she didn't want to be found.

Moving toward the stairs, he decided to wish her well before returning to the polo fields, hoping to catch the last match if he was lucky. His footsteps echoed on the hardwood floor as he walked toward the master suite. Her scent met him the moment he stepped onto the landing. It was an alluring fragrance that he knew all too well, and it was so much a part of her that he couldn't imagine her wearing any other perfume.

Jamming his hands into his pockets, he continued his stroll. This would be the first time he'd be here without her. He shook off the dreary feeling that realization had brought on. He was a big boy and could handle it. Besides, Carmen had done enough damage to mess up his life. He doubted he would ever forgive her for breaking his heart, for making him believe there was such a thing as true love and then showing him there really wasn't.

He'd stopped trying to figure out at what point they'd begun drifting apart. He would be the first to admit he'd spent a lot of hours working, but all those hours he'd spent away from her were meant to build a nice nest egg so they wouldn't have to work forever.

And although she was paid well for her movies, as her husband, he'd still felt it was his duty to make sure she got anything and everything she wanted in life. They had talked about having a family, but she hadn't understood that knowing he could provide for her and any child they had was important to him.

Her parents had had money and unlike him, she hadn't grown up poor. More than anything, he'd wanted to keep her in the lifestyle she'd been accustomed to. What in the world could be so terribly wrong about wanting to do that? To this day he just couldn't figure it out, and the more he thought about it, the angrier he got.

He had built his world around her. She had been the only thing that truly mattered and everything he'd done had been for her. But she hadn't appreciated that. So now, because of a decision she'd made without him, he was a man whose life was still in turmoil, although he fought like hell to keep that a secret. And he placed the blame for his shattered life at her feet.

He reached the bedroom's double doors and without bothering to knock, he pushed opened the door.

And stopped dead in his tracks.

Three

Carmen swung around at the sound of the bedroom door opening and tightened her bathrobe around her. She threw her head back, sending hair cascading around her shoulders. "What are you doing in here, Matthew?"

For a moment he simply stood there staring at her, no doubt taking in the fact that she had just taken a shower and was probably stark naked beneath her short robe.

When he didn't answer, she said in a sharp tone, "Matthew, I asked you a question."

His attention shifted from her body and slid up to her face. "What do you think you're doing, Carmen?"

His voice sounded strained and his breathing shallow. "What does it look like I'm doing? I just finished taking a shower and now I'm putting on clothes. You should have knocked."

Carmen watched as something flickered in the depths of his dark eyes and a muscle clenched in his jaw. He took his hands out of his pockets, causing the material of his pants to stretch across the huge bulge at his center. It was quite obvious he'd gotten aroused from seeing her half-naked. She inwardly smiled. He'd taken the bait just the way she'd planned.

"I own this place. I don't have to knock, Carmen. And why are you still here? Why aren't you gone or at least packing?"

She crossed her arms over her chest and followed the movement of his eyes from her face to her breasts. She was very much aware that her curves were outlined through the silky material of her robe. It seemed he was very much aware of it, as well.

"I decided that I won't be leaving."

He pulled his gaze away from her chest. "Excuse me?"

"I said I won't be leaving. I'd assumed you would be in L.A. all summer, which is why I made plans to spend my vacation here. I don't intend to change that just because you've shown up."

A muscle clenched in his jaw again, making it obvious her statement hadn't gone over well with him. She wasn't surprised when he said, with an icy gaze, "You should have checked my plans for the summer. If you had, I would have told you this place was off-limits. I regret that you didn't. I also regret that you have to leave."

She inched her chin a little higher and declared, "I'm not going anywhere, Matthew. I deserve some peace and quiet. I've worked hard this year."

"And you don't think that I have?"

The sharpness of his tone had her gearing up for a fight. But she had to be careful what she said or he would toss her out and halt her plan. "I know you work hard, Matthew.

In fact, you carry working hard to the extreme," she said bluntly.

His gaze narrowed and she wondered if perhaps she'd pushed him too far. But she couldn't help saying how she felt. The amount of time he'd spent away from her would always be a wound that wouldn't heal.

He began moving toward her in that slow, precise walk that could make women drool. She wished she didn't notice his sex appeal or just how potently masculine he was. She had to get a grip. Her objective was to make him regret ever taking her for granted, to give him a taste of his own medicine, so to speak. She intended to turn her back on him like he'd done to her.

Carmen swallowed when he came to a stop in front of her but she refused to back up—or down.

"You," he said with deep emphasis, "are not staying here. I think things were pretty clear in the divorce settlement. You wanted to end our marriage and so you did. Under no circumstances will we stay under the same roof."

Carmen saw the hardness in his features. This face that once looked at her with so much love was staring at her with a degree of animosity that tore at her heart.

"Then nothing is different, Matthew, since we seldom stayed under the same roof anyway. I'm not leaving. I was almost mobbed by the paparazzi getting here and they are probably hanging around like vultures waiting for me to leave. Your recent love life has caused quite a stir and they are trying to bait me into giving my opinion."

"The media isn't giving me any more slack than they're giving you. And your affair with Bruno Casey isn't helping matters, either. I'm sure if you return to California, he'll be able to put you up for the summer in that place he owns off the bay."

It was on the tip of her tongue to tell him nothing was

going on with Bruno, but she decided it was none of his business, especially in light of his ongoing affair with Candy. She refused to bring the other woman up since the last thing she wanted was for him to think that she cared. Which she didn't.

"Bruno is shooting in Rome and this is where I want to be. I love it here. I've always loved it here and the only reason you didn't agree to let me have this place during the divorce was because you knew how much I wanted it. For spite, you were intentionally difficult."

"Think whatever you like. I'm leaving to catch the last of the polo matches. I want you gone when I return."

"I'm not leaving, Matthew."

His expression turned from stony to inexplicably weary. "I'm not going to waste my time arguing with you, Carmen."

"Then don't."

They stood there staring at each other, anger bouncing off both of them. Then, without saying another word, Matthew turned and walked out. Carmen held her breath until she heard the front door slam shut behind him.

Matthew decided not to return to the Seven Oaks Farm for the match. Instead, he went for a drive to clear his head and cool his anger. Carmen was being difficult—she hadn't behaved that way since the early days of their courtship.

He had pursued her with a single-minded determination he hadn't known he was capable of, and she had put up a brick wall, refusing to let him get close. But he'd known the first moment he'd laid eyes on her that he not only wanted her to star in his movie but he wanted her in his bed and wouldn't be satisfied until he got both.

She'd gotten the part in the movie, earning it fair and square. Getting her into his bed had proven to be difficult and before he got her there, he'd realized he had fallen in love with her. He wasn't certain how it had happened, but it had. He'd loved her so deeply, he knew he wasn't capable of ever loving another woman that way.

She'd stood before him in that church and promised to love him forever. So what if he worked long hours—didn't "till death do us part" mean anything to her? And if he hadn't worked so hard, he would not have earned the reputation of being one of the country's up-and-coming film producers.

A throbbing warmth flowed through his chest, which was immediately followed by a rush of anger that was trying to consume him. He had wanted so much for them and she had done something so unforgivable it hurt him to think about it. He had been absolutely certain she was the one person who understood his drive to build something of his own, the one person who would never let him down. His father had let him down by not marrying his mother when she'd gotten pregnant, and then his mother had let him down when she married Charles Murray, the stepfather from hell. Carmen had restored his faith that there was someone out there who wouldn't disappoint him. So much for that.

Matthew parked the car on the side of the road and just sat there, gazing at the beach. Walking into the bedroom and seeing her barely clothed had been too much. For a moment, lust had overshadowed his common sense and he could only think of how her breasts felt in his hands, how they tasted in his mouth.

With the sunlight streaming through the window, her nearly transparent robe had revealed the darkened triangle between her legs. It had taken all his strength not to cross the room, toss her on the bed and bury himself deep inside her body the way he used to after they'd argued and made up.

And they'd had to make up a lot since the amount of time he'd spent away from home had always been a bone of contention between them. But they'd always worked through it. What he'd tried so hard to figure out was, what had made the last time different? Why had she felt like throwing in the towel? She'd known his profession when she married him. As an actress, she of all people should have understood how things were on a set. Her filing for divorce had confused the hell out of him.

He remembered the night he hadn't shown up in Spain as planned. It had been a week from hell on the set. Wayne Reddick, the main investor for the movie he'd been producing at the time, had unexpectedly shown up on location. He and Wayne had butted heads several times and the man's impromptu visit had prompted him to cancel his plans to meet Carmen in Barcelona. The fate of his production, which had been behind schedule, was at stake and it had taken some serious talking for the man to agree to extend funds for the movie's completion. He had tried calling Carmen to explain things, but she hadn't answered the phone. The next thing he knew he was receiving divorce papers.

He tightened his hand on the steering wheel thinking that maybe he was handling the situation with his ex-wife all wrong. Since she was hell-bent on staying in the Hamptons, maybe he should just let her. It would give him the chance to extract some kind of revenge for the hell she'd put him through.

He glanced at his watch. A smile touched his lips when he pulled back onto the road and headed home, determined to return before she left. He needed to convince her that it was fine with him if she stayed, without making her suspicious of his motives.

He'd been an actor before becoming a director and producer. He would seduce her back into his bed and then make her leave. And he would go so far as to change the locks on the doors if he had to.

The more he thought about it, the more he liked the idea and knew just how he could pull it off. When it came to seduction, he was at the top of his game.

Four

"You're still here, Carmen."

Carmen drew in a quick breath before turning around where she stood in the kitchen. Matthew had said he was returning to the polo matches—she hadn't expected him back so soon. At least she'd had time to put on some clothes and start dinner.

"I told you that I'm not leaving, Matthew. I deserve my time here so I figure you can do one of two things."

"Which are?"

She was surprised he asked. "You can call the cops and have me arrested for trespassing, which should make interesting news this week. Or you can leave me be and ignore the fact that I'm here. This house is big enough for you to do that."

She studied his features for some clue as to which option he fancied. And then he said impassively as he leaned against the kitchen counter, "The latter will cause just as much ruckus as the former."

He was right about that. Ever since she had publicly thanked him when receiving her Oscar, the tabloids had claimed a reconciliation between them was in the works. The paparazzi had shadowed their every move, determined to find out if the rumors were true and the Hollywood darlings were ready to kiss and make up. And then her agent had come up with this idea to make things even more interesting by introducing Bruno into the mix. Plus there was the matter of his lingerie model.

"I'm sure when you explain things to Candy, she'll understand," she said with warm humor in her voice. Of course Candy wouldn't understand, but then Carmen really didn't give a royal flip. Candy had had her eyes on Matthew for years and hadn't wasted any time latching on to him after their divorce had become final.

He stared straight into her eyes when he asked, "And what about Bruno? Is he an understanding sort of guy?"

The heat of his gaze touched her in a way that she couldn't ignore. She knew he meant to be intimidating and not sexual, but that look was as sexual as anything could get and she wasn't happy about the surge of desire flowing through her. The memories of what usually followed such a look swirled all around her and touched her intimately. Bottom line, Matthew Birmingham could make her feel like no other man could.

"Must be pretty serious if you have to think about it."

She blinked upon realizing he'd been waiting for her response while she was thinking that he could still take her breath away. "Yes, he's an understanding sort of guy." She would let him ponder exactly what that said about the seriousness of their relationship.

Carmen turned to check the rolls she had put in the oven

earlier. She was wearing a pair of jeans and a tank top. He'd always liked how jeans hugged her backside, and she was giving him an eyeful now as she bent over. She heard the change in his breathing and inwardly smiled. Poor baby, he hadn't seen anything yet.

"If I decide to let you stay," he was saying behind her, "there have to be rules."

She turned around and lifted a brow. "What kind of rules?"

"Bruno isn't welcome here."

She could live with that, since she hadn't intended to invite him anyway. "And what about *your* Miss Candy? Will you respect me as your former wife and keep her away while I'm here?"

It annoyed her that he actually had to think about his answer. Then he said, "I guess our plans can be rearranged."

A coldness settled in her heart. His response meant two things. He *had* intended to bring Candy here, and the two of them were sleeping together. The latter shouldn't surprise her since she of all people knew how much Matthew enjoyed making love. That was the one thing the two of them had in common.

"Does that mean you're okay with me staying, Matthew?"

"Seems you're hell-bent on doing that anyway. And like you said, the less the media knows about our business, the better."

She laughed. "You're concerned with the media? You? The same person who kissed me in front of a tent filled with people, including Ardella Rowe?"

"Like I said, you kissed me first." He looked over her shoulder at the stove. "So, what are you cooking?"

"Something simple."

"I didn't know you could cook at all." The amused glint in the dark depths of his eyes made her smile, as well. Matthew didn't smile often but when he did, it was contagious—and sexy.

"I started cooking after Rachael Ray had me on her show." And then, because she couldn't help it, she added, "I'd prepared a couple of meals for you when I thought you would be coming home. When you never showed up, I fed everything to the garbage disposal."

He looked at her as if he wasn't sure she was serious. "Here's another rule, if we're going to be here together. No talk of the past. You bailed out on our marriage and I'd rather not get into it—"

"I wasn't the one who bailed out, Matthew," she countered, lifting her chin. "You replaced me."

A fierce frown covered his face. "What the hell are you talking about, Carmen? I was never unfaithful to you."

"Not in the way you're thinking," she said, truly believing it. "But there *was* a mistress, Matthew. Your work. And she was as alluring to you as any woman could be. I couldn't compete and eventually stopped trying."

His frown deepened. "I don't want to hear it. I've heard it all before."

He'd heard, but he hadn't listened. "Fine," she said, "then don't hear it because personally, I'm tired of saying it. "

"You don't have to say it. We're divorced now."

"Thanks for reminding me."

There was a moment of awkward silence between them, although the chemistry they shared was keeping things sizzling. She knew he felt it as much as she did, and wasn't surprised when he tried easing the tension by asking in a civil yet curious tone, "What are you making?"

She glanced over at him. "I've smothered pork chops

with gravy and got some rice going along with homemade rolls and field peas."

"You prepared all that?"

"Yes. I made more than enough—you're welcome to dig in, too. Later we can toss for the bedroom."

He raised a brow. "Toss for the bedroom?"

"Yes, toss a coin to see which one of us will get the master suite, and who will have to settle for one of the guest rooms."

He shrugged. "Save your coin, I don't mind using the guest room. I'm going to wash up."

Carmen watched him walk out the kitchen, thinking that while revenge might be sweet, she needed to watch her step where he was concerned, especially since all she had to do was look at him to remember how things used to be between them—both in and out of bed. But for some reason she was reminded more of how things were in bed than out. It didn't take much for sensuous chills to flow through her body whenever he was near, even during those times she found him infuriating.

A wave of uneasiness washed over her. It was too late to question whatever had possessed her to take him on since it was too late to back off now. And the one thing she did know was that she would not go down in defeat.

"I never got the chance to thank you for mentioning me at the Academy Awards during your acceptance speech," Matthew said, glancing across the table at Carmen as they ate. "You didn't have to do that."

He hadn't expected her to give him any kind of acknowledgment when she'd accepted her award. He'd figured, considering how things had been during the divorce, that his name would be the last one off her lips that night. It had been quite a surprise. But then, she was always surprising him, like when he'd returned from washing up to find she'd set the table for two.

"Of course I did, Matthew," she claimed. "Regardless of how and why our marriage ended, I would not have taken that role if it hadn't been for you. You made me believe I could do it."

He didn't say a word as he thought back over that time. He'd known she could do it and along with Bella Hudson-Garrison, who was cast as the lead, Carmen had given a stellar performance. Bella had walked away with an Oscar for best actress, and Carmen won best-supporting actress.

He had arrived at the Kodak Theater and walked the red carpet alone, surprising many by not having a woman on his arm. His manager, Stan, had tried convincing him to bring a date, since chances were Carmen would be bringing one. But he hadn't taken Stan's advice. And when he saw Carmen had also come alone, he'd been happy, although he'd tried convincing himself he didn't give a damn.

He'd felt bitter that night, knowing she should have strolled down the red carpet on his arm. And she'd looked absolutely radiant; her gown had been stunning. On that night for a brief moment, he had placed his anger aside and had rooted for her getting the award she truly deserved. And when she had unselfishly acknowledged him as the driving force behind her taking the part, the cameras of course had switched to him, to gauge his reaction. His features had remained emotionless but on the inside, he had been humbled by what she'd done.

"So, Matthew, what's this new business venture you're involved with here in New York?"

He blinked, and realized he'd been staring at her like a fool. He quickly glanced down at his wineglass to get his bearings and recoup his common sense. When he felt pretty sure he had done both, he responded, "You know that although I enjoy doing features, it's always been my dream to make a documentary."

Carmen had known that. While married, they had talked about his dream many times.

"Well, earlier this year I learned that New York is gearing up to celebrate the one hundred and twenty-fifth anniversary of the Statue of Liberty's dedication, and that the city is looking for someone to film a documentary highlighting the event. The last big documentary was directed by Ken Burns back in 1986, and it was nominated for Best Documentary Feature."

She nodded. "That was a while ago."

"My name was given to the committee, and I've met with them several times over the past year. I learned yesterday that I was selected. They've requested that I use a New York–based film crew, and I don't have a problem with that. It only means I need to be here for preproduction, not in L.A. It's important that I get to know the people I'll be working with and they get to know me and my style."

She knew just what he was talking about. Matthew was an outstanding director, dedicated to his work and he expected those who worked with him to be dedicated, as well. She'd been in two of his movies and both times had been in awe of his extraordinary skills.

A sincere smile touched her lips. She was happy for him. In fact, she was ecstatic. God knows he'd worked hard to prove himself in the industry, which was one of the reasons why they were sitting across the table from each other not as husband and wife but as exes. Still, she would put the bitterness aside and give him his due.

"Congratulations, Matthew, that's wonderful. I am truly happy for you," she admitted, standing and carrying their plates to the sink.

"Thank you," Matthew said, leaning back in his chair, steepling his fingers together as he watched Carmen move across the room with more grace than any woman he knew. There was a jaw-dropping sexiness to her walk that had the ability to turn on any man, big time—especially him.

It hit him just how much he missed seeing her and spending time with her. The last time they'd been together had been in the judge's chambers, ending their marriage with their attorneys battling it out to the end.

"So, you're committed to being here all summer then?" she asked, turning around, leaning against the counter and meeting his gaze.

He smiled, wondering what she would do if she knew he was practically stripping her naked with his eyes while thinking of all the naughty things he wanted to do to her body. "Yes."

"Working?"

"Basically."

"Which means I'll rarely see you."

Matthew flinched. She knew how to say things that could make him grit his teeth. She made it seem as if he'd never given her any attention while he worked. Well, that was about to change. He was on a mission to seduce her and then kick her out on that hot little behind of hers.

"Maybe you will and maybe you won't. There will be days when I'll be working from here."

She shrugged. "It doesn't matter, Matthew. Work drives you no matter when and where you're doing it. That's all you ever think about."

He could tell her that wasn't true since at that very moment, he was thinking about how he wanted to make love to her once he got her back in his bed. "If that's what you want to believe."

She laughed shortly. "That's what I know. Now, if you don't mind, I intend to go to bed."

He shot her a confused look. "Bed? Don't you think it's kind of early? The sun's still up," he pointed out.

She lifted a brow. "And your point?"

My point is that I can't very well seduce you if you are making yourself scarce. "There's still time to do things tonight."

"I agree, which is why, after putting on my pj's, I plan to sit out on my bedroom balcony with a good book and watch the sun set over the ocean. I might go for a swim in the pool later tonight, but you shouldn't be concerned that I'll be underfoot. Like I said, this house is big enough for both of us. See you later."

She turned and left the kitchen. He watched her go, admiring her body, remembering her touch, more determined than ever to get her in his bed.

Five

Carmen curled up on the chaise longue on the private balcony off the master suite. If she were going to seduce Matthew, the last thing she needed to do was appear too accessible, too anxious to be in his presence. That was the reason she'd decided to go to her room first rather than straight to the pool.

A cool breeze was coming in off the ocean. She recalled making love with Matthew on this very balcony one night that first year he had brought her to the Hamptons. She had been concerned that their neighbors would see them, but Matthew had assured her that they had total privacy. The house had even been built in a no-fly zone, which kept the overzealous paparazzi from taking to the skies.

She glanced at the book she'd placed on the table, a romance novel she had been trying to get through for the last couple of days. It's not that it wasn't a good book—it was—but it was hard to read about someone else's fantastic love life when hers had gone so badly.

Instead of resuming the book, she decided to close her eyes and conjure up her own love story with her and Matthew in the leading roles. Things between them had been romantic during the early days of their marriage, especially that first year when he hadn't wanted her out of his sight. They had been in bed more than they had been out. Matthew was something else in the bedroom—he'd been able to reach her on a level that went deeper than any man ever had—and a part of her knew that no other man ever would.

From the moment they'd met, something had passed between them that was instinctive, and primitive. She was surprised she'd been able to read her lines during the audition session. That day, for the first time in her life, she'd discovered how it felt to truly desire a man.

She had gotten the role because Matthew had seen something in her. He thought she was good, and was going places. Although the temptation to become his lover during filming had been great, she had been determined to keep things professional between them.

After they'd wrapped the movie, they had their first date. He had taken her someplace simple—his favorite bar and grill for hamburgers, fries and what he'd claimed was the best milk shake she would ever taste. He'd been right. That night had practically sealed her fate. They'd dated exclusively for six months and then that Christmas, he'd asked her to marry him and she'd said yes.

The media had kept tabs on their budding relationship, referring to them as Hollywood's Darlings—Matthew, the staunch bachelor who claimed he would never marry, and she, the woman who'd stolen his heart. Their courtship had been as private as they could make it, but that hadn't stopped the paparazzi from stalking their every move and painting them as the couple whose marriage was most likely to succeed in Hollywood. Boy, had they been wrong.

Nearly five years later and here they were, no different than most other Hollywood couples—divorced and blaming the other for what had gone wrong. She drew in a deep breath, not wanting to think of how she'd felt being replaced by his career. The loneliness and pain had nearly swallowed her whole. Although by that time she'd had success as an actress, as a wife she felt like a total failure—a woman who couldn't compete against her husband's workaholic nature, who couldn't entice him away for a smoldering-hot rendezvous.

More pain settled around her heart as she remembered she'd lost more than her husband's attention in Barcelona. She'd also lost the child they had made together. Had she gone full-term, their little girl or boy would have been almost four months old by now.

She felt her lip trembling and fought back tears. She wanted to recall the good things about their marriage. She wanted to remember how well they'd gotten along in the beginning, how she would respond to just about anything when it came to him. His soft laugh, his touch, the sound of his breathing…that look he would give her when he wanted to make love.

She had seen that same look in his eyes today in the kitchen. She didn't know what racy thoughts had been going through his mind, but her body had responded and a rush of sensations had flowed through her. Her hormones had surged to gigantic proportions and it would have been so easy to cross the room, slide onto his lap, curl into his arms and bury her face in the warmth of his chest. Then she would have kissed him the way she used to. Kissing him had the ability to make her all but moan out an orgasm. In fact, a few times she had done that very thing.

She had the satisfaction of knowing he wanted her. Although she was woman enough to admit she'd desired him, too. What she had to do was keep her desires at bay while continuing to stir up his. That was her game plan and she intended to stick to it. She would not get caught in her own trap.

But there was nothing wrong with getting wrapped up in memories while lying stretched out on a chaise longue with the breeze from the ocean caressing her skin. Memories were a lot safer than the real thing. With her eyes still closed, she vividly recalled the night when she and Matthew had come out here, naked and aroused, with only one thing on their minds.

They had gone to a polo match and returned home, barely making it up to their bedroom to strip off their clothes. And then he had swept her off her feet and carried her to the balcony. Even now she could recall how fast her heart had been beating and how her pulse had throbbed. Pretty similar to how she was feeling now, just thinking about it.

He'd reached out to touch her breasts and her stomach had automatically clenched in response. Then she had watched in heated lust as he'd leaned forward and used his tongue to capture a nipple between his lips and—

"Carmen? Why didn't you answer when I knocked?"

She found herself staring into a pair of dark, sensuous eyes. His lips were so close to hers that it wouldn't have taken much for him to lean in just a little closer and taste her. And then there was his scent—aftershave mingled with man—that began manipulating her senses in a way that could be deemed lethal.

Her eyes narrowed as she felt a warming sensation

between her thighs. Matthew was crouched down over her. She fought to ignore the sensual currents that were rippling through her.

"What are you doing here?" she asked, her voice sounding strained to her own ears.

His gaze continued to hold hers. "I knocked several times and you didn't answer."

The heat of his breath was like a warming balm to her lips. She was tempted to lick the fullness of his mouth from corner to corner. It didn't exactly surprise her that she was thinking of doing such a thing, considering what she'd been thinking about just moments ago.

She slowly pulled herself up in a sitting position, causing him to move back, for which she was grateful. The last thing she needed right now was to be in close proximity to him. The temptation was too great. "And why were you knocking on the bedroom door when I told you I would be out here on the balcony reading?" she asked.

"I need to get my things moved to the guest room." He paused a moment and said, "I noticed you were sleeping, but figured I could get my things without disturbing you. But then…"

She lifted a brow. "But then what?"

A sensual smile touched the corners of his lips when he said, "But then I heard you say my name in your sleep."

She faltered for a minute, then quickly fought not to show any emotions as she swung her legs to the side to get up, causing him to back up a little more. She stared at him, exasperated, not sure what she should say. She decided not to say anything at all. What was the use in denying such a thing? It probably hadn't been the first time she'd said his name in her sleep and more than likely it wouldn't be the last. After all, he'd once had the ability to make her come just by breathing on her. In fact, he probably still could.

"Go ahead and get your things, Matthew. I'm awake now," she said, breaking eye contact with him to stand and gaze toward the ocean. He could think whatever he liked about hearing her say his name. She figured all kinds of thoughts were running through his mind—he was probably trying to figure out the best way to get into her panties right now.

She glanced back at him and her nipples immediately hardened when she noticed how he was staring at her outfit. She had changed into a strapless terry-cloth romper and it fit real tight over her backside. She knew just how much he enjoyed looking at that part of her anatomy.

He also used to compliment her on what he said was a gorgeous pair of legs. And now he was scanning her from head to toe, and concentrating on the areas in between. He wasn't trying to hide his interest.

"Is there a problem, Matthew?" she asked, watching his gaze shift from her legs to her mouth. Seeing his eyes linger there ignited a burning sensation low and deep in her belly.

His survey then slowly moved up to her eyes. A flash of panic ripped through her when she recognized the *let me make you come* look in his eyes. She felt her body succumbing without her consent.

"There's no problem, if you don't think there's one, Carmen," he said throatily, her name rolling sensuously off his tongue.

"I don't," she replied, easing back down on the chaise longue, knowing he was watching her every move. She stretched in a way that caused his attention to be drawn to her backside and legs once again. "I'm sure you don't need my help packing up your things."

Too late she realized she'd said the wrong thing. His expression went from hot to furious. She knew he was recalling the last time she'd said those very words to him, when he was moving out of their home in Malibu.

"You're right, Carmen. I didn't need your help then and I don't need it now."

Six

As Matthew began opening drawers to collect his clothes, he had to keep reminding himself there was a reason he hadn't yet tossed his ex-wife out on her rear end.

When she hadn't opened the bedroom door, he'd figured she had fallen asleep on the balcony. He thought he could be in and out without waking her. But when he'd heard her moan his name, not just once but several times, nothing could have stopped him from going on that balcony.

He had found her stretched on the chaise with her eyes closed, wearing a hot, enticing outfit that barely covered her. Seeing her resting peacefully had tugged at his heart, while her clothing and her words had tugged on another part of his anatomy. He'd stood there, thinking about all the things he'd love to do to her while getting harder as the seconds ticked by.

And he had been tempted to kiss her, to make love to her mouth in a way that would not only leave her breathless but tottering on the brink of a climax. When she had awakened and looked into his eyes, he had seen a need as keen as any he'd ever known from her. And then she had ruined the moment by reminding him that they were no longer husband and wife, and wouldn't be sharing the same bedroom or bed.

But not for long.

He was looking forward to reminding her just what she'd been missing this past year. And the way he saw it, she was definitely missing something if she was moaning his name in her sleep.

As he pulled the briefs and socks out the drawer and tossed them into the bag on the bed, he glanced to the balcony where Carmen now stood with her back to him, leaning against the rail and gazing out at the ocean again. At that moment, intense emotion touched him and nearly swelled his heart while at the same time slicing it in two.

He had loved her and he had lost her. The latter should not have happened. She should have stuck by him and kept the vows they'd made to each other. But when the going got tough, she got going.

He pushed the drawer closed, deciding to put his plan into action. She had pushed a few of his buttons—now it was time for him to push a couple of hers.

Carmen felt Matthew's presence before he'd even made a sound. She felt a unique stimulation of her senses whenever he was near. She had felt it earlier today when he'd entered the tent at the polo match. She'd known he was there. Just like she knew he was here now.

Biting her bottom lip, her fingers gripped tight on the rail as her breathing quickened, her pulse escalated and heat flowed through her. He didn't say anything. She couldn't stand another second of silence and slowly turned around.

The sun had gone down and dusk had settled in. Behind him she saw the light from the lamp shining in the bedroom but her focus was on him. She studied him, not caring that it was obvious she was doing so. His eyes darkened and she felt his desire. And as she stood there, she couldn't help but relive all the times he had held her in his arms and made love to her.

He had been the most giving of lovers, making sure she enjoyed every sexual moment they'd shared to the fullest. Her body was tingling inside, remembering how it felt to have his mouth to her breasts, or how his lips could trail kisses all over her body, heating her passion to the highest degree. It had been her plan to get him to the boiling point, but she was ashamed to admit he had her there already.

She pulled in a deep breath. "Are you done?"

"Not quite."

And then he slowly crossed the distance separating them. "I came to say good-night."

The husky sound of his deep voice sent sensuous shudders running all through her. Total awareness of him slid down her spine. She forced her gaze away from his to look out at the ocean to say something, anything to keep her mind off having her way with him.

"I love it here, Matthew. Thanks for agreeing to let me stay." She glanced back at him and saw he'd come to stand directly beside her. "You didn't have to, considering the terms of our divorce," she decided to add.

He stared at her for a moment and then said, "It was the right thing to do. At the very least, we can be friends. I don't want to be your enemy, Carmen."

His words nearly melted her, but she had to remember that she wanted him to regret the day he began taking her for granted, to realize that when she'd needed him the most, he hadn't been there for her. She had been alone while grieving their loss.

"What are you thinking about, Carmen?"

She glanced up at him. "Nothing."

"Maybe I should give you something to think about," he said softly, in a deep, rich voice. And then he wrapped his arms around her waist and lowered his mouth to hers.

She saw it coming and should have done a number of things to resist, but it would have been a waste of time and effort. Every part of her turned to mush the moment his lips touched hers. When his tongue began mingling with hers, she moaned deep in her throat.

Carmen hadn't known how much she'd missed this until now. She had tried burying herself in her work so she wouldn't think about the loneliness, the lost passion, the feel of being in the arms of the one man who could evoke sensations in her that kept her wet for days.

I miss being with the one man who can make me feel like a woman.

He deepened the kiss and she felt the rush of sexual charge. And when he lowered his arms from her waist to cup her backside, bringing her closer to him, she felt the hardness of his huge erection pressing into her. On its own accord, her body eased in for a closer connection.

Their mouths continued to mate in the only way they knew how, a way they were used to. But regardless of the number of kisses they had shared in the past, she was totally unprepared for this one. She hadn't expected the degree of desire or the depth of longing it evoked, not only within her but within him, as well. She could feel it in the way his tongue dominated her mouth as if trying to reclaim what it once had, and was entitled to. He was not only taking what she was giving but going beyond and seizing everything else he could.

Then he began slowly grinding his body against her. She felt the hot throb of his erection between her legs as if the fabric of their clothing wasn't a barrier between them. His body rubbing against hers electrified her senses in a way that felt illegal. And how he fit so perfectly between her legs reminded her of just how things had been with them, whether they were standing up or lying down, in a bed or stretched out on top of a table. They'd always made love with an intensity that left them with tremors of pleasure that wouldn't subside for hours.

Everything around her began to swirl wildly, and as his large hands continued to palm the cheeks of her backside, pressing her even closer to him, an ache took over in the pit of her stomach and began spreading through every part of her.

He slowly released her mouth but didn't stop the movement of his body as he brushed kisses across her cheekbones and chin. She pulled in a deep breath and then released a whimpered sound of pleasure from deep in her throat as he licked a path from one corner of her mouth to the other.

Blood rushed through her veins and it took everything within her to keep from begging for more. But nothing could stop the waves of pleasure and the tremors that began to shake her. She closed her eyes and reveled in the sensations rushing through her, bit by glorious bit. And when he began nibbling on her lips and then proceeded to suck those lips into his mouth, she was literally thrown over the edge. She pulled her mouth from his and cried out as intense pleasure shook her to the very core while he continued to grind his body against hers with a rhythm that had her rocking in sensuous satisfaction.

"That's it, sweetheart, let go," he murmured against her moist lips. "You are totally beautiful when you come for me. So totally beautiful. I miss seeing that."

And she missed feeling it, she thought, as the orgasm that had ripped into her slowly began receding and returning her to earth after a shuddering release. And when she felt the heat of his tongue lap the perspiration from her brow, she slowly opened her eyes.

"Matthew."

His name was a breathless whisper from her lips. As if he understood, he leaned down and kissed her, tenderly but still with a hunger she could feel as well as a taste she could absorb.

He slowly pulled his mouth away and with a sated mind, she met his eyes. The gaze staring back at her was just as intense and desirous as earlier, making it obvious that although she'd easily managed a climax fully clothed, he'd maintained more control over his aroused state.

"Matthew, let me—"

He placed a finger to her lips to halt whatever she'd been about to say. "Good night, Carmen. Sweet dreams."

She watched him leave, thinking that thanks to him, her dreams tonight would be the sweetest she'd had in a long time. She had to admit that this was not how she had planned for things to go with Matthew. He had deliberately tapped into one of her weak spots, which was something she hadn't wanted to happen. Was he gloating that he'd gotten the upper hand?

Carmen drew in a deep breath as her body hummed with a satisfied sensation. A flush heated her cheeks when she remembered how he had kissed her into an orgasm; she was feeling completely sated. The chemistry between them was just as it had always been, explosive.

She leaned back against the rail and knew, even though

the sexual release had been just what she needed, she had to regroup her priorities and continue with her plans. Everyone was entitled to get off the track at least once, but the important thing was to get back on. And she was confident that after a good night's sleep, she would be back in control of her senses once again.

Seven

Pulling off his shirt, Matthew headed for the bathroom, needing a shower. A cold one. Just the thought that he had brought Carmen pleasure had nearly pushed him over the edge. While kissing her, he had been overtaken with a raw and urgent hunger. The sensation had been relentless, unyielding, and for him, nearly unbearable.

As soon as his lips had touched hers, the familiarity of being inside her mouth had driven him to deepen the kiss with a frenzy that had astounded him. And each time she had moaned his name, something deep inside him had stirred, threatening to make him lose all control.

It didn't take long after she'd bailed out of their marriage to realize that she was the only woman for him. Any time he held her in his arms, kissed her, made love to her, he'd felt like a man on top of the world, a man who could achieve and succeed in just about anything. He had worked so damn hard to make her happy and in the end all of his hard work had only made her sad.

He stripped off his clothes, filled with a frustration he was becoming accustomed to and a need he was fighting to ignore. He stepped in the shower and the moment the cold water hit, shocking his body, he knew he was getting what he deserved for letting a golden opportunity go by. But no matter the torment his body was going through, he was determined to stick to his plan, and at the moment he was right on target.

His goal was to build up a need within her, force her to remember how things were between them, and how easily they could stroke each other into one hell of a feverish pitch. And then when she couldn't handle any more, when she was ready to take things to another level, instead of sweeping her off her feet and taking her to the nearest bed like she would expect, he would show her the door.

He stepped out of the shower and was toweling himself dry when he heard his cell phone ring. Wrapping the towel around his middle, he made his way over to the nightstand to pick it up. Caller ID indicated it was his manager, Ryan Manning.

"Yes, Ryan?"

"It would have been nice if you'd given me a heads-up that you and Carmen were back together."

Matthew frowned. "We're not back together."

"Then how do you explain the photograph the *Wagging Tongue* plans to run of the two of you kissing? Luckily I have a contact over there who thought I'd be interested in seeing it before it went to press. They plan to make it front page news that the two of you have reconciled your differences and are remarrying. The papers hit the stands tomorrow."

Matthew rolled his eyes. The *Wagging Tongue* was one

of the worst tabloids around. "Carmen and I are divorced, nothing has changed."

"Then what was that kiss about?"

"It was just a kiss, Ryan, no big deal. People can read into it whatever they want."

"And what about Candy?"

"What about her?"

"What will she think?"

Matthew drew in a deep breath and said, "Candy and I don't have that kind of relationship, you know that."

"But the public doesn't know that, and this article will make her look like a jilted lover."

He had no desire to discuss Candy or their nonexistent bedroom activities. Ryan knew the real deal. Candy was trying to build a certain image in Hollywood, and Matthew had agreed to be Candy's escort to several social functions, but only because he had gotten sick and tired of hanging around the house moping when he wasn't working. Ryan and Candy's agent felt it would be good PR. He'd known the media would make more out of it than there was, but at the time he hadn't given a damn.

"And where is Carmen now?" Ryan asked.

"In bed." He smiled, imagining the erroneous vision going through his manager's mind.

"Dammit, Matthew, I hope you know what you're doing. Her leaving almost destroyed you."

A painful silence surrounded him. No one had to remind him of what he'd gone through. "Look, Ryan, I know you mean well, but this is between me and Carmen."

"And what am I supposed to tell the media when they can't contact you and then call me?"

"Tell them there's no comment. Good night, Ryan."

Matthew breathed a sigh of relief as he ended the call. Ryan could be a pain in the ass at times, especially when it came to the images of his clients. But then he could definitely understand the man's concerns. His separation and subsequent divorce from Carmen had left him in a bad way for a while. But that was then and this was now. He could handle things. He could handle her. Pride and the need for self-preservation would keep him from falling under her spell ever again. He felt good knowing that although he'd given her some sexual release, she would still go to bed tonight needing even more. There was no doubt in his mind she would be aching for his touch.

He smiled. This sort of revenge was pretty damn sweet.

The next morning Carmen was easing out of bed when her cell phone rang. She reached over and picked it up. The sunlight pouring through the window was promising a beautiful day.

"Hello?"

"Girl, I am so happy for you. When I saw that article and picture, I almost cried."

Carmen recognized the voice of her good friend Rachel Wellesley. Rachel was a makeup artist she'd met on the set of her first movie. The close friendship she and Rachel had developed still existed to this day.

She knew what Rachel was referring to and decided to stop the conversation before her friend went any further. Carmen was well aware that Rachel probably said a special prayer each night before she went to bed that Carmen and Matthew would reunite. Rachel liked taking credit for playing matchmaker and initially getting them together.

"Chill, Rachel, and hold back the tears. No matter what you've heard, seen or read, Matthew and I aren't getting back together."

There was silence on the other end of the line.

"But what about the kiss that's plastered all over the front page of the *Wagging Tongue* this morning?" Rachel asked, sounding disappointed. "And don't you dare try to convince me it's a photo that's been doctored."

Carmen didn't say anything as she remembered the kiss and the effect it had on her. "No, it's not a photo that's been doctored, although a part of me wishes that it were. It started when I ran into Ardella Rowe at the polo match yesterday and she mentioned something about Matthew and me being enemies. I firmly denied it and went further, painting a picture of the two of us as friends, regardless of what the tabloids were saying. Well, before I could get the words out of my mouth, Matthew walked into the tent and all eyes were on us. To save face, I greeted him with a kiss on the cheek. Of course he decided to take advantage of the situation by turning a casual kiss into something more."

"From the photo, it looked pretty damn hot, if you ask me."

It was. But it was nothing compared to the one they'd shared last night on the balcony. She felt heat rise to her face as she imagined what he'd thought of the fact that she'd climaxed from his kiss.

"You should talk to him, Carmen, and tell him the truth. You know what I think about you not telling him about losing the baby."

Carmen pulled in a deep breath. Rachel was one of the few people who knew about what had happened that night. When she'd found out about her pregnancy, she'd been so excited she had wanted to share it with someone. Rachel had actually been the one who'd come up with the idea of making a surprise video telling Matthew of her pregnancy.

While curling up in his arms on the sofa in the villa, she

had planned to suggest that they watch a few video pitches for possible projects that directors had sent her. Instead, unbeknownst to him, she would play the video of her first ultrasound, even though the baby was just a tiny speck in a sea of black.

But things hadn't worked out that way.

"Yes, I know how you feel and you know how I feel, as well. Matthew should have been there with me." He'd always had legitimate excuses why he was late arriving someplace or not able to show up at all because of some last-minute emergency on the set. But for once he should have placed her above everything else, and he hadn't.

Knowing that Rachel would try to make her see Matthew's side of things, reminding her that he had no idea what was going on, she quickly said, "Look, Rachel, let me call you back later. I'm just getting up."

"Sure. And where's Matthew?"

"I have no idea. We spent the night under the same roof but in different bedrooms, of course. Knowing him, he's probably gone by now. He has this new project here in New York, so I'm sure he's left already to go into the city."

"The two of you will be living there together all summer?" Rachel asked.

Carmen could hear the excitement in Rachel's voice. She knew it would be a waste of time telling her not to get her hopes up because it wasn't that kind of party. The guest room Matthew was using was on the other side of the house, and considering his schedule, their paths would probably only cross once or twice while they were there.

"Yes, for the most part, but this house is so big I doubt I'll even see him."

After ending her conversation with Rachel, Carmen got up and went into the bathroom. She planned to go swimming in the pool and then head down to the beach after breakfast.

Even though things had started off pretty rocky between her and Matthew yesterday, thanks to him she'd slept like a baby last night. An orgasm brought on by Matthew Birmingham never failed her. Whenever she'd had a tension-filled day on the set, he would make love to her to calm her frazzled nerves.

But upon waking her greedy body wanted more. It was as if she'd suddenly developed an addiction to Matthew's touch, a touch she had managed to do without for more than a year but was craving like crazy now.

An intense yearning and longing was rolling around in the pit of her stomach and although she was trying to ignore it, doing such a thing wasn't working. Now that her body recognized the familiarity of his touch, it seemed to have a mind of its own.

She frowned while stripping off her nightgown. She wondered if Matt had deliberately set her up for this—she wouldn't be surprised to discover that he had. He of all people knew how her body could react to him. So, okay, she would admit that he had bested her this round, but she was determined not to lower her guard with him again.

Eight

"I thought you had left to go into the city." Matthew glanced up and nearly swallowed his tongue. Carmen was standing in the kitchen doorway dressed in a two-piece bathing suit with a sheer, short sarong wrapped firmly around her small waist that placed emphasis on her curvaceous hips and beautiful long legs. Her hair was pulled up into a knot displaying the gracefulness of her neck, and even from across the room he could smell her luscious scent.

He felt a flash of anger with himself that she could still have this kind of effect on him. But last night had proven just how things were between them. Of course sex had never been the issue—her inability to believe she was the most important thing in his life had been. What he resented most was her not giving them time to work anything out. And once the media had gotten wind of their problems, they had made a field day of it, printing and stating things that hadn't been true.

But seeing her now almost made it impossible to recall why there were problems between them. She was the most beautiful, desirable woman he had ever laid eyes on.

He lowered his head and resumed eating. It was either that or do something real stupid like get up from the table, cross the room and pull her into his arms.

"I figured since you have business to take care of in Manhattan, you would have left already," she explained, looking genuinely surprised to see him.

He wondered if she'd actually been hoping their paths would not cross today, and he knew that was a pretty good assumption to make. Sighing, he picked up his coffee cup. "Sorry to disappoint you, but I'll be doing most of my work from here."

"Oh," she said. He continued to watch her as she crossed the room to the stove.

"I take it you're spending the day on the beach?" he asked, wondering why she had to look so ultra-feminine and much-too-sexy this morning. But then she always looked good, even when she'd just woken up in the morning. He'd so enjoyed making love to her then, stroking the sleepiness from her eyes as he stroked inside her body.

"Yes, that's my plan, after taking a dip in the pool first," she said, pouring a cup of coffee. She took a sip and smiled. "You still make good coffee."

He chuckled as he leaned back in his chair. "That's not the only thing I'm still good at, Carmen."

Carmen swallowed hard, thinking that he didn't have to remind her of that.

Her heart began pounding in her chest and she felt breathless when he stood. All six feet three inches of him was well built and dangerously male. And she thought now what she thought the first day she'd laid eyes on him: Matthew Birmingham had the ability to ignite passion in any woman.

Focus, Carmen, focus. Don't get off track here. You need to win back the upper hand. Remembering her call from Rachel, she asked, "Has Candy Sumlar called you yet?"

He pushed his chair under the table and went to the sink, pausing for a moment to glance at her. "Is she supposed to?"

Carmen shrugged. "Don't be surprised if she does. Someone took of picture of us yesterday and it made the front page of the *Wagging Tongue*."

He turned toward her after placing his cup in the sink. "I know. It could cause a problem or two, I suppose."

He took a few steps toward her until Carmen had to tilt her head back to look up into his face. "Then why did you kiss me?" she asked.

"Because I wanted to."

His words, precise and definitely unapologetic, gave her a funny feeling in the pit of her stomach. Sexual tension filled the room and for a moment, she was mesmerized by his gaze—those extraordinary dark eyes could render a woman breathless if she stared into them for too long.

So she broke eye contact and moved away. "Doing things that you want to do without thinking about the possible outcome can get you in trouble."

"And who said I didn't think about it?"

Carmen fell silent. Was Matthew insinuating that he'd kissed her knowing full well what he was doing? That he would have done so anyway, even if she hadn't made a move first with that kiss on the cheek? She ignored the tingle in her stomach at the mere thought that this was more than a game to him. That perhaps he had wanted her and initiating that kiss had been just the thing to push him over the edge.

Umm. The thought of that had her nipples feeling hard and pressing tight against the bikini top. She drew in a deep breath and as her lungs filled with the potent air they were both breathing she felt her nipples grow even more sensitive. He was leaning against the counter, his eyes roaming up and down her body. She wanted him to check her out good and assume that he could get more from her than just the hot-and-heavy kiss they'd shared last night. Then she would gladly show him how wrong that assumption was. If he was playing a game, she would show him that two could play.

She moved toward the table to sit down, intentionally swaying her hips as she did so. She took a sip of her coffee as she felt heat emitting from his gaze.

"There are some muffins in the refrigerator if you want something else to go with your coffee," he said.

"Thanks, I'm fine."

"There's another polo match tomorrow. Do you plan on going?" he asked.

"I do," she replied.

She knew why he was asking. By tomorrow, a number of people would have read the article and all sorts of speculations would be made. The main question was, how would they handle it?

The room got quiet. He finally broke the silence by asking, "What about Bruno? Will he get upset when he hears about the article?"

Carmen looked over at him and plastered a smile on her lips. "No, because he knows he has nothing to worry about." She knew that comment irked him. Back in the day when he'd been a movie star, Matthew and Bruno had been rivals as Hollywood heartbreakers. The two never developed a close friendship and even now merely tolerated each other for appearance's sake.

"Good. I wouldn't want to cause friction between the two of you."

"You won't." Seeing she would not be able to drink her coffee in peace while he was around, she stood and announced, "I'm going to the pool."

Matthew watched her leave, irritated by what she'd said about Bruno knowing he had nothing to worry about. The very thought that the man was that confident about their relationship didn't sit well with him. A sudden picture of her in Bruno's arms flashed through his mind and he felt anger gathering in his body, all the way to his fingertips.

He drew in a deep breath and then let it out slowly, wondering what Bruno would think if he knew his girl had gotten pleasured by her ex last night. Although they hadn't made love, Matthew knew her well enough to know that that orgasm had been real and potent. In fact, if he didn't know any better, he'd think it was the first she'd had in a while, which meant Bruno wasn't taking care of business like he should.

But the thought of that man taking care of business at all where Carmen was concerned had steam coming out of his ears and a tic working in his jaw. Deciding it was time to rev up his plans of seduction a notch, he left the kitchen to go upstairs to change.

Carmen opened her eyes when she heard footsteps on the brick pavers. She took one look at Matthew and wished she'd kept them closed. He was walking toward her wearing a pair of swim trunks that would probably be outlawed if worn in public.

Her gaze settled on his face and the intense expression she saw there, before lowering her eyes to the sculpted muscles of his bare chest and then sliding down to his midsection. The waistband of his trunks hung low and fully outlined a purely masculine male.

She stiffened slightly when she felt a deep stirring in the middle of her stomach and fought to keep perspective. She sat up on the chaise longue and held his stare, wishing her heart would stop beating so rapidly.

And wishing she still didn't love him like she knew she still did.

That stark realization had her moving quickly, jumping out her seat, nearly knocking over a small table in her haste. "What are you doing here, Matthew?"

He came to a stop in front of her. "Why do you always ask me that like I'm out of place or something?"

Silence hung heavy between them. Then she lifted her chin and said, "Probably because I feel like you are. I'm not exactly used to having you around." She then moved toward the pool.

Matthew didn't say anything, mainly because he was focused on the pain in her voice—as well as the realization that she was right. This *was* the longest they had been together in the same place in a long time—including when they were married.

Suddenly, he couldn't even fortify himself with the excuse that all those hours he'd been away working had been for her. Because in the end, he'd still failed to give her the one thing she'd wanted and needed the most: his time.

He had missed this—her presence, the connection they'd shared in the beginning but had somehow lost in the end. How could he have been so wrong about what he thought she truly wanted and needed? He had wanted them both to find happiness, but they sure as hell weren't happy now. At least, he wasn't. His stomach clenched at the thought of just how unhappy he was. His plan for revenge didn't taste as sweet as it had yesterday, and he had no idea what to do.

He watched as she stood by the pool, untying the sarong from around her waist and dropping it to the ground. And then she dove in, hitting the water with a splash. He stood watching her, remembering when all he'd wanted was to make her his wife and to have children together one day. He had loved and wanted her so much.

And I still love her and want her.

The admission was like a sharp punch to his gut. Nothing mattered at that moment—not the humiliation he'd felt when she left, nor the anger or frustration he'd suffered when she chose to file for a divorce. What he was sure about more than anything was that he wanted her and if given the chance to repair the damage, he would handle things differently. What he was unsure about was whether or not she wanted another go with him. There was one way to find out.

It was time he was driven by a different motivation, not of revenge but of resolution. He moved toward the pool and dived in after her.

It was time to get his wife back.

Nine

Carmen surfaced when she heard a big splash behind her. Seeing Matthew in the water, she decided it was time to get out of the pool and began swimming toward the other side.

She eased herself out to sit on the edge and watch him, studying his strokes, meticulous and defined, and the way he was fluidly gliding through the water. He was an excellent swimmer, of course—after all, he had attended UCLA on a swimming scholarship.

He swam toward her until he was right there, treading water between her legs. And before she could catch her next breath, he reached up and pulled her into the water.

"Matthew!"

Carmen wrapped her arms around his neck so she wouldn't go under, but that ended up being the least of her worries as he tightened his hold on her and pressed his mouth to hers. She whimpered when his tongue grabbed hold of hers, stroking it hungrily. And when he deepened the kiss, she automatically wrapped her legs around his waist, feeling the strength of his thighs and his hard erection through his wet swim trunks.

She returned the kiss, realizing that she was powerless to resist this intense interaction, this outburst of sexual chemistry and reckless behavior. Heat and pressure were building up inside her. The feel of the water encompassing them captivated her, making her all too aware of the way he knew exactly what to do to her.

He began licking and nibbling around her lips, and she knew instinctively that this was a man with outright seduction on his mind. The only thing wrong was that she was supposed to be seducing him, not the other way around.

She couldn't resist the urge to clamp her mouth down on his, needing the feel of his tongue tangling with hers. She could truthfully say she'd never enjoyed kissing a man more—she had missed this intimate foreplay tremendously. Though she hated to admit it, being here with him was long overdue and she needed it like she needed to breathe.

When he began wading through the water toward the steps, she saw they'd somehow made it to the shallow end. Pulling his mouth from hers, he shifted her body in his arms as he walked up the steps from the pool. Cool air brushed across her wet skin and her entire body shuddered in his embrace.

She didn't ask where they were going. It didn't matter. She was overwhelmed by the way he was staring down at her with every step he took. And when he placed her on the lounger, she reached out, not ready for him to release her.

"I'm not going anyplace," he whispered in a deep husky

tone, running his hands along her wet thighs. "I'm just grabbing a couple towels to dry us off."

He only took a step or two away from her but Carmen instantly felt desperate for his touch. The loneliness of the past year loomed over her and she felt a stab of regret, wishing she had handled things between them differently.

She had known from the first that Matthew was a proud man, a man who'd had to work hard for anything he'd ever had in life. That was the reason he was so driven. When they'd married, he had vowed to take care of her and in his mind, working hard was the only way to do that. And although she'd told him over and over that all she wanted was him, he hadn't been able to hear her, mainly because he was who he was—a man determined to take care of his own.

At that moment, something in her shifted and she felt something she hadn't felt in a long time—peace and contentment. When he returned to her with the towels, she reached up and touched his face, tracing his lips with her fingertips before leaning in and kissing him softly on the mouth.

She felt his hold tighten and she detected the raw hunger within him, but he let her have her way. Knowing he was holding back caused a surge of desire to flood every part of her body.

She released his mouth and he wrapped her up in one of the towels, wiping her dry. She moaned in total enjoyment over the feel of the soft terry cloth against her flesh. He slid the towel all over her body to absorb the water from her skin, leaving no area untouched. She knew she was being lured into a temptation she could not resist.

He dried himself off, as well, and she watched, enjoying every movement of the towel on his body, looking at his chest and shoulders and legs. He was so well built—watching him had to be the most erotic thing she'd witnessed in a long time.

Tossing the towels aside, he leaned down and covered her mouth with his once more while stretching out to join her on the lounger, her body under his. He broke off the kiss and used his teeth to lift her bikini top. Before she could utter a sound, his mouth was at her breasts, sucking the hardened tips of her nipples between his lips.

Matthew had always enjoyed her breasts and that hadn't changed. Carmen could tell that he refused to be rushed while cupping the twin globes in his hands, using his mouth to tease them one minute and lavish them the next.

And then she felt him tugging at her wet bikini bottoms, removing them from her body and tossing them aside. He stepped back and began lowering his swim trunks down his legs.

She shifted on the lounger to watch him like she'd done so many other times. Her breath caught at what a fine specimen of a man he was in the raw—she had always enjoyed seeing him naked. And at that moment she was filled with a need to pay special tribute to his body the way she used to.

When he moved toward her, she sat up and her mouth made contact with his stomach as she twirled her tongue all around his abs. She felt the hard muscles tense beneath her mouth, and her hands automatically reached out to clutch his thighs as the tip of her tongue traced a trail from one side of his belly to the next, drawing circles around the indention of his belly button.

He moaned her name. Pressing her forehead against his stomach, she inhaled the scent of him. She then leaned back, her face level with his groin. She reached out and grabbed hold of his shaft, feeling the aroused member thicken even more in her hands.

The dark eyes staring down at her were penetrating, hypnotic and displayed a fierce hunger she felt all the way in the pit of her stomach. Although he wouldn't verbally express his desires, she knew them. She had been married to him for three years and she knew exactly how to pleasure him in a way that would give him the utmost gratification.

She opened her mouth and leaned forward, her lips and tongue making contact with his erection. She heard his tortured moan as she greedily licked him all over, focusing on her task as if it were of monumental importance—and to her, it was. He was the only man she'd ever performed this act on, and she derived just as much pleasure giving it as she knew he was getting from it.

"Carmen."

Her name was a guttural groan from his lips and when she felt his fingers plunge into her hair, she slid his erection inside her mouth and went to work, just the way he'd taught her, the way she knew that could push him over the edge. She so enjoyed watching him fall.

The thought that she was driving him crazy was a total turn-on for her. As her mouth continued its torment, she could feel his pleasure heightening. Soon, the same heat and passion consuming him began taking hold of her. He was the only man who could make her bold and daring enough to do something like this, the only man who made lust such a significant thing.

Was it wrong to desire her ex-husband so much? He was the very man who had broken his promise to make her the most important thing in his life, to cherish her forever....

She pushed those thoughts to the back of her mind, not wanting to dwell on all the things that had gone wrong.

Instead she wanted to dwell on him, on making love with the most irresistible man to walk the face of the earth.

"Carmen!"

The throaty sound of her name on his lips—the instinctive response of a man reaching extreme sexual pleasure—pulled her back to the here and now. When the explosion she'd been expecting happened, she was overwhelmed by her own passion and the depth of her love for him.

And then she felt herself being lifted into his arms. When he crushed his mouth to hers, she knew there was no stopping either of them now. Their wants and desires were taking over and they wouldn't deny themselves anything.

She wrapped her arms around his neck as she felt herself being carried up the winding stairs. She knew exactly where he was taking her—to the master suite, their bedroom, their bed.

She pulled in a deep breath when they reached their destination and he eased her out of his arms and onto the bed. Before she could draw in another breath, he was there with her, reaching out to her and pulling her back into his arms.

His hands touched her everywhere, and where his hands stroked, his mouth soon followed. He moved from her lips down past her neck to her chest where, after cupping her breasts in his hands and skimming his fingertips across them, he used the tip of his tongue to lavish the twin mounds and hardened tips.

Matthew then glided his hands down her hips and between her legs to cup the warmth of her womanhood. And then his mouth was there, pressing against her feminine folds, as if needing the taste of her on his tongue.

"Oh, Matthew."

She rocked her body against his mouth and he responded

by plunging his tongue deeper inside of her. The sensations he was evoking were so intense she could only cry out in a whimper once more before pleasure erupted within her, spiraling her into a shattering climax, the intensity of which brought tears to her eyes.

"You liked that?" he asked moments later when he slid back up her body and began licking her neck.

Unable to speak, she nodded her head. His mouth claimed hers again. Moments later he straddled her body with his arms, inching her legs apart with his knees. When he released her mouth, he peered down at her. "You sure about this, baby?" he whispered hoarsely before moving any farther.

She hadn't been more sure about anything in her life. "Yes, Matthew, I'm sure."

That was all he needed to hear. He continued to hold Carmen's gaze as his body lowered onto hers, his thick erection moving past her feminine folds and deep into the core of her. Her inner muscles clutched him and he groaned her name. He had missed this. He had missed *her*. He wanted to close his eyes and relish the feeling of being inside her this way, but he kept his eyes open. He held tight to her gaze as he continued moving deeper and deeper inside of her as she lifted her hips to receive all of him.

And when he'd buried himself in her to the hilt, he let out a rugged growl as pinnacles of pleasure began radiating through him starting at the soles of his feet and escalating upward. He felt every single sensation as he moved, his strokes insistent as he thrust deep, fully intent on driving her wild, over the edge and back again.

"Matthew, please…"

The longing in her voice revealed just what she was

asking for and his strokes increased to a feverish pitch, giving her just what she wanted. He understood her need, comprehended her desires since they were just as fierce as his own. He thrust deeper still as they moved in perfect rhythm.

She tightened her legs around his back when he groaned, triggering an explosion that ripped through their bodies. As he spilled into her, he lowered his mouth to hers and took her lips while an earth-shattering release tore through them.

He sank deeper and deeper into her as a pulsing ache took control of his entire body and he felt himself swelling all over again inside her. Moments later, another orgasm slashed through him, drowning him in waves after waves of intense pleasure.

The moment he released her mouth, she cried out for him. "Matthew!"

As she gazed up at him, he knew their lovemaking had proven what they'd refused to admit or acknowledge up until now, this very moment.

Divorce or no divorce, their life together was far from over.

Ten

Depleted of energy, Carmen lay still with her eyes closed, unable to move, her body still intimately connected with Matthew's. She could feel the wetness between her thighs where their bodies were still joined.

She slowly opened her eyes. Matthew's face was right there. He was asleep, but still holding her in his arms, his leg was thrown possessively over her, locking their entwined bodies together. It was as if he'd deliberately chosen that position so that he would know if she moved the slightest bit.

She glanced at the clock on the nightstand and saw that it was close to two in the afternoon, which meant they had spent the last five hours in bed. Closing her eyes again, she thought that she had never experienced anything quite like the lovemaking session they'd just shared, and she could still feel remnants of sexual bliss simmering through her.

Her body quivered at the memory of his mouth between

her legs, and of his tongue lapping her into sweet oblivion. She hadn't made love with another man since their divorce and now she knew why—her body didn't want anyone other than Matthew.

Suddenly, she felt him starting to swell inside her. She opened her eyes to stare right into the darkness of his. They lay there, gazing at each other while his shaft expanded into a huge, hard erection.

"Oh my goodness." The words slid from her lips as she felt him stretching her inside. Her inner muscles clamped tight and wouldn't let him go.

He leaned forward and kissed her, moving in and out at a slow pace. His unhurried strokes eased the tremendous ache between her legs and matched the rhythm of his tongue as it mingled with hers. She couldn't help moaning with each thrust into her body as she was overtaken with desire. He was so painstakingly thorough it nearly took her breath away.

Moments later she pulled her mouth from his when her body erupted into an orgasm so intense she screamed in ecstasy, totally taken aback at the magnitude of pleasure ripping through her. And then Matthew followed her into the thrill of rapture as his body exploded, as well. As he drove harder and deeper, she could actually feel his release shoot right to her womb.

"Matthew…"

She moaned his name from deep within her throat and when his mouth found hers again, she continued to shudder as her body refused to come down from such a rapturous high.

"I can't believe I feel so drained."

Matthew glanced over at Carmen and smiled. They had just arrived at Ray's Place, a popular hangout on the

Hamptons. She was leaning against his car and, dressed in a pair of jeans and a cute pink blouse, she was looking as breathless as she sounded. "I wonder why," he said.

She laughed and gave him a knowing look. "Oh, you know exactly why, Matthew Birmingham." She raked a hand through her hair and laughed again before saying in a somewhat serious tone, "You're pretty incredible."

His smile widened. "You're pretty incredible yourself. Come on, let's go grab something to eat to feed that depleted soul of yours." He took her hand in his and they headed toward the entrance of the establishment.

The one thing he'd always enjoyed about Ray's Place was that it was private and the paparazzi were not allowed on the grounds, which was probably why a number of people were there tonight, many of whom had ventured to the Hamptons for the polo matches.

Another thing he liked abut Ray's Place was the excellent service, and he appreciated that they were seated immediately. He glanced over at her and thought he didn't mind being guilty of making her tired. Making love to her most of that day had been the most erotic thing he'd done in a long time, and because it was her and no other woman, it had been special.

"Umm, so what do you think we should order?" she asked, looking at the menu.

He leaned back in his chair. "Whatever can fill me up. I'm starving."

She rolled her eyes. "You're famished and I'm exhausted. Go figure."

"My friend Matthew Birmingham and his lovely wife, Carmen. How are you?"

Matthew glanced up and smiled. "Sheikh Adham, I heard you were a guest this year at the Polo Club. How are you?" he asked, standing and shaking the man's hand. He had met the sheikh over ten years ago when, as a college student, the sheikh had visited the United States and participated in a swimming competition at UCLA. They had become good friends then.

"I am fine, Matthew." And he leaned over and kissed Carmen's cheek. "And you, Carmen, are as beautiful as ever."

"Thanks, Sheikh Adham," Carmen said, smiling.

The man then gestured to the woman by his side. "And let me introduce my wife, Sabrina. Sweetheart, Matthew and Carmen are friends of mine."

The woman smiled as she greeted them. Matthew fought not to show the surprise on his face. Adham married? The woman was certainly a beauty. But he'd spent some time with Adham just last year while working on a historical piece in the Middle East when he'd claimed marriage was the furthest thing from this mind. Matthew couldn't help wondering what had happened to make him change his mind.

"Would you and Sabrina like to join us?" Matthew heard Carmen ask.

Adham shook his head. "We appreciate your kindness but we've already eaten and were just leaving. Hopefully, we can get together soon after one of the polo matches."

"Carmen and I would like that." They chatted for a few more minutes before the couple left.

"Wow, I can't imagine Adham married," Carmen said, speaking aloud what Matthew's thoughts had been earlier. Matthew returned to his seat, remembering it was well-known that Adham used to have a wild streak and be quite a womanizer.

"They look happy," Carmen added.

Matthew wasn't so sure about that. For some reason he didn't quite feel that happiness that Adham and Sabrina were trying so hard to emit.

"I can't believe I ate so much," Carmen said when they returned from dinner.

She glanced over her shoulder and saw Matthew grinning as he tossed his car keys on the table. "And just what do you find so amusing?" She couldn't help but ask him.

He leaned back against the door. "I have to say I don't ever recall seeing you eat that much. You ate your dessert and mine."

Carmen chuckled as she dropped down on the sofa. "Only because you didn't seem as hungry as you claimed you were. I, on the other hand, was not only exhausted, I was hungry."

He nodded. "Are you full now?"

"Yes, pretty much so."

"And your energy level?"

She lifted a brow, wondering why he wanted to know. "Good. Why?"

"Keep watching, you'll figure it out."

And she did. First went his shirt, which he removed and tossed aside. His shoes and socks came next and Carmen watched fascinated. When his hand went to the zipper of his jeans she shivered in anticipation. The man had a body that could make her tremble while waiting for it to be bared.

Determined not to be undone, she eased off the sofa and began removing her own clothes. By the time she had tossed her last article of clothing aside, he was slowly moving toward her. "You're slow, Carmen."

She grinned. "And you look hard, Matthew."

"You're right," he said, pulling her into his arms.

She groaned out loud with the feel of his naked body against hers.

"Haven't you gotten enough yet?" she asked, smiling.

"No. Have you?"

She wrapped her arms around his neck. "No."

And then he pulled her back down on the couch with him.

Matthew gazed up at the ceiling. If anyone had told him that he would be spending a good part of his entire day making love to his wife—his ex-wife—he would not have believed it. Even now, while lying flat on his back, trying to regain his strength and listening to her moving around in the bathroom, he was still somewhat stunned.

Their lovemaking had been off the charts as always, but something had been different—he'd detected another element in the mix. An intense hunger had driven them to new heights, making them fully aware of what they'd gone without for twelve months and just how much they longed to have it back.

He had assumed leaving the house awhile would wean some of their sexual hunger, but it hadn't. No sooner had they returned, they were at it again. He could not get enough of her, and they had gotten it on every chance they got. Without any regrets. At least there certainly hadn't been any on his part and he hoped the same held true for her.

What if she was not feeling the same way that he was? What if it had been lust and not love that had driven her to sleep with him, and now that she had, nothing had changed for her?

Shifting positions, he lay on his side with his gaze fixed on the bathroom door. Carmen was an actress, and a damn good one, but when it came to certain emotions, he could read her like a book. At least he used to be able to.

But today she had made love with him as if they hadn't just spent an entire year not talking to each other. He wished he could let the matter go, but he couldn't. Their love had been too strong for him to just let things continue as they had before. He didn't want revenge anymore. What he wanted more than anything was an explanation as to why she had ended their marriage. As far as he was concerned, they could have worked it out if she'd just given him a chance, if she'd just communicated with him.

He drew in a deep breath as he waited for his ex to come out of the bathroom. It was time for all cards to be placed on the table. It was time for her to be honest with him and for him to be honest with her, as well. He wanted his wife back, and it was time he told her so.

Carmen stood at the vanity mirror after her shower, staring at her face, hoping that Matthew would still be asleep when she left the bathroom. She was not ready to see any sign of regret in his eyes. It had probably just been lust driving him to make love to her like that, and now that it was out of his system, it would be business as usual with them. He would remind her, in a nice way of course, that they were still divorced and nothing had changed.

Boy, was he wrong. Something had changed—at least it had for her. She could no longer deny that she still loved him. And she had to tell him about the baby—it wasn't fair to keep it a secret anymore.

At the time, she had been so hurt that all she'd wanted to do was wallow in the pain without him. She'd blamed him for not being there that night and had even gone so far as to tell herself that if he had been there, things might have been different. She hadn't wanted to believe what the doctor had said—that a large percentage of women miscarry a baby at some point during their reproductive years. According to the doctor there was no reason for her not to have a normal pregnancy when she was ready to try again. But at the time, she hadn't wanted to think about another pregnancy. She'd only wanted to mourn the one she'd lost.

She wished she'd handled things differently. She should have called Matthew and let him know what happened. She knew deep down that there was nothing, work or otherwise, that would have kept him from hopping on the next plane to Barcelona to be with her.

He would have held her while she cried, kissed her tears away and told her everything would be okay, that as soon as she was ready they would make another baby. He would have meant every word.

And when she'd been able to travel he would have taken her home and cared for her, pampered her and shown her that no matter how many hours he spent away from her, she was the most important thing in his life.

He had told her that many times but she hadn't wanted to hear it even though she, of all people, knew his family history and knew that taking care of her was important to him. But what she had done was turn her back on him and without telling him the full story, she had filed for a divorce. She hung her head, ashamed of her decision. He probably hated her for doing that, and their relationship could be beyond repair at this point.

She lifted her face to stare at her reflection again. Yesterday, she'd wanted to seduce her ex-husband in the name of revenge, but today she knew she needed him in her life. She loved him and wouldn't be happy until they were together again.

Somehow she needed to make him fall in love with her

all over again. But first she had to tell him the truth. She had to tell him about the baby.

Matthew held his breath when the bathroom door opened and the moment Carmen appeared in the doorway his heart began pounding deep in his chest. The sunlight pouring in through the windows seemed to make her skin glow.

Silently he lay there and studied the way her short silk bathrobe clung to her curves. He had every reason to believe she was naked underneath it. There was a damp sheen to her brown skin and her hair was tied back away from her face, emphasizing her eyes and mouth. As he continued to watch her, that mouth he enjoyed kissing so much slowly curved into a sexy smile.

There were no regretful vibes emitting from her and he let out a relieved breath as they stared at each other. They'd done that a lot lately, staring at each other without saying anything. But what he saw in her gaze now nearly melted his heart. She loved him. He was certain of that. He might not ever hear her say the words to him again but he could see it—it was there on her face, in her eyes and all around those delectable lips.

He intended to do whatever had to be done to remind her of what they'd once had. More than anything, he wanted her to accept that there was nothing the two of them couldn't work out together. That was the one thing he was certain about. Two people couldn't love each other as deeply as they did and still stay apart. In his book, things just didn't work out that way.

He watched as she slowly moved across the room toward him and he sat up to catch her when she all but dived into his arms. And then she was kissing him with a hunger and need that he quickly reciprocated. He fought for control, his body burning with a need that was driving him off the deep end. He wanted to do nothing more than bury himself inside her body.

Moments later, she ended the kiss and leaned back. Her robe had risen up her thighs and the belt around her waist was loose, giving him a glimpse of a tantalizing portion of her breasts and the dark shadow at the juncture of her legs. The scent of her was drawing him in, making him remember how he'd felt being inside of her.

Unable to resist, he reached out and slid his hands beneath the silk of her bathrobe and began stroking her breasts, letting his fingertips tease the hardened nipples. When he began moving lower, she whispered, "Matthew, let's talk."

He agreed with her. They should talk. He wanted to start off by telling her how he felt, but the moment he opened his mouth to do so, he realized he wasn't ready after all. He didn't want to revisit the past just yet. Instead, he wanted to stay right here, right now. "I'm not ready to hash out the bad times, Carmen. Right now I just want to forget about what drove us apart and only concentrate on this, what has brought us together."

He held her gaze, knowing as well as she did that there was no way they could totally forget. If this was about nothing but sex, then that was one thing, but deep down he knew it wasn't. The love between them was still there, which meant there were problems they needed to address. Had his long hours been the only thing that had driven her away from him? He was certain she knew he hadn't been unfaithful to her.

She nodded, and he drew in another deep breath. Eventually they would talk, and he meant really talk. Because now that he had his wife back in his arms, his heart and his bed, he intended to keep her there.

Eleven

Carmen had agreed to postpone their conversation at Matthew's request, and they had spent an amazing week together, enjoying each other. They were both fearful that an in-depth discussion of the state of their affairs would put them back at square one. And they weren't ready to go back there yet.

Instead they'd opted to spend time together, living in the present and not venturing to the past. At the polo matches, everyone was speculating as to what exactly was going on between them. And the *Wagging Tongue* wasn't helping matters. More than one snapshot of them together had appeared in the tabloid, and she and Matthew didn't have to work hard to figure out the identity of the person passing the photos to the paper. Ardella Rowe was the prime suspect. They had seen her at dinner the same night they'd run into Sheikh Adham, and she had tried pestering them with questions, which they'd refused to answer.

At one polo match, she and Matthew had stuck to "no comment" when a mic was shoved in their faces by a reporter wanting to know whether or not they'd gotten back together. The fact of the matter was, they couldn't exactly answer that question themselves.

One paper she had seen claimed they were having a summer fling with no chance of reconciliation while another had announced they'd remarried at a church on Martha's Vineyard. A third had even reported the real Carmen Akins was in Rome with Bruno and the woman Matthew was spending time with in the Hamptons was only a look-alike, a woman he'd taken up with who closely resembled his ex-wife. She could only shake her head at the absurdity of that.

Carmen stood at the huge window in the library, looking out upon the calm waters of the Atlantic.

This past week had been the best she'd known. And it hadn't bothered her in the least the few times Matthew had gone into Manhattan on business, even when one of those meetings had extended well into the late afternoon.

Now she could truly say that although she'd blamed him for the breakup of their marriage, a good portion of the blame could be placed at her feet. She of all people knew how demanding things could be for a director at times, dealing with temperamental actors, overanxious investors and too-cautious production companies. On top of that, there were a number of other issues that could crop up at a moment's notice. And because she'd known all of that, was aware of the stress, she could have been a lot more understanding and a lot less demanding of his time.

The sad thing about it was that she'd always been an independent person and had never yearned for attention from anyone, yet during that time she'd needed Matthew's. Or she'd thought she did. And when she'd lost the baby, she couldn't stand the thought of a future in which Matthew was never there for her, not even when she needed him most.

She selected a book of poetry and was sitting down in one of the recliners when she heard Matthew's footsteps on the hardwood floor. She glanced up the moment he walked into the room, surprised. He had taken a ferry to Manhattan that morning and she hadn't expected him back until much later.

The moment their eyes met, a sensation erupted in the pit of her stomach. And then the craving began.

She placed the book aside as he walked toward her with that slow, sexy saunter. She knew exactly what he had on his mind. Because it was on hers, too. But she also knew it was time for them to talk. They couldn't put it off any longer.

Carmen rose from her seat. "I think it's time for us to talk now, Matthew. There's something I need to tell you."

Matthew had a feeling he knew what Carmen wanted to talk about but he wasn't ready to hear it. The last thing he wanted to discuss was that she was beginning to feel as if there were nothing but sex between them. Given that they'd made love multiple times during the day for seven straight days, he could certainly see why she thought that.

But what she'd failed to take into consideration was that every time he was inside her body, his heart was almost ready to burst in his chest. And each and every morning he woke up with her in his arms made him realize just how much he loved her. What she didn't know was that making love to her was his way of showing her with his body what he hadn't yet been able to say out loud.

He knew things couldn't continue this way between

them. Time was running out and they would have to talk sometime, would have to rehash the past and decide what they would do about their future. But not now, not when he wanted her so much he could hardly breathe.

"Matthew, I—"

He reached out and pulled her into his arms, and within seconds surrender replaced her surprise. This is what he wanted. What he needed. He deepened their kiss, intending to overtake her with passion, to overwhelm her senses.

He closed his arms tightly around her and lifted her just enough to fit snug against his crotch, needing to feel her warmth pressed against him. The feel tormented him and he pulled his mouth away, turning her around so her back fit solidly against his chest.

"Hold on to the table, baby," he whispered.

Carmen felt the warmth of his breath on her ear and knew Matthew was trying to take her mind off her need to talk. And for now, she would let him. Her insides began to quiver and she pressed against him. Emotions she couldn't hold at bay consumed her entire being.

"I want you so much I ache," he added in a deep husky voice that had her body shivering. She loved him and wanted more between them than this. But she would settle for this for now. She didn't want to think about what would happen when she told him about losing their baby. Would he understand the reason she hadn't told him?

He slid his fingers into the elastic of her shorts and pulled them down her legs, leaving her bare. The cool air hit her backside and when he began using his hands to caress her, molding her flesh to his will, she couldn't help but moan even more.

She heard the sound of his zipper and then he tilted her hips up to him. She closed her eyes to the feel of the warm hardness of his erection touching her while his fingers massaged between her legs.

She tightened her grip on the table as he placed the head of his shaft at her womanly folds. The feel of him entering her from behind sent her mind spinning and when he pushed deep, she cried out as sensations tore through her. In this position she felt a part of him, enclosed in his embrace, in the comfort and protection of his body.

He began moving and her body vibrated with every stroke inside her. She closed her eyes, relishing the feel of something so intimate and right between them. He ground his hips against her, going deeper and deeper—she wondered if they would be able to separate their bodies when the time came to do so.

When he slid his hands underneath her top and began fondling her bare breasts, she threw her head back. She loved the feel of his hands on her breasts, the tips of his fingers tormenting her nipples.

The way he was mating with her, the hot warmth of his breath on her neck as he whispered all the things he planned to do to her before the night was over—all of that stirred heat and stroked her desire to a feverish pitch she could barely contain any longer.

She let go, sensations ripping through her. She began quivering in an orgasm from head to toe. Those same sensations overpowered him and he tilted her up toward him even more and drove deeper inside of her. He groaned her name as she felt his hot release. She felt it. She felt him. And before she could stop herself, she cried out, "I love you, Matthew."

She couldn't believe she'd said it, and part of her hoped that he hadn't heard it. Slowly, he turned her around and gave her the most tender, gentle kiss she'd ever had from him. But he didn't say anything. Not a word.

* * *

Matthew glanced around the bedroom as he leaned against the closed door. The last thing he had expected was for Carmen to admit to loving him, and as soon as he could escape her presence, he had. He should have told her that he loved her, too, but for some reason he hadn't been able to do so. Not that he didn't, but because he loved her so much. Had he confessed it at that moment he probably would have lost it—to know that she still loved him after all this time was more than he could handle. He needed to pull himself together before facing her. Before pouring his heart out to her and letting her know just how miserable his life had been without her in it.

He'd enjoyed being here with her for the past week and was looking forward to the rest of the summer. And he was doing a pretty good job balancing the work and spending time with her. They'd spent a lot of hours on the beach and had gone to several polo matches. And of course the media was in a frenzy trying to figure out what was going on between them.

Even with all the gossip floating around, things between them were almost like they'd been in the beginning. But not quite. He knew his time was running out. Given what she'd just said to him, they had to talk. And they had to talk today. He would take her for a walk on the beach, and they would finally hash it all out.

He opened a drawer and searched around for his sunglasses, smiling when he found the case buried at the bottom. He was about to close the drawer when he noticed a DVD case labeled, "For my Husband." And it was dated the day he was supposed to meet her in Spain.

Curious about the video, he took it out the drawer. After inserting the DVD into the player, he sat on the edge of the bed.

He smiled when Carmen appeared on the screen in what looked like a spoof of his very first job as a director, which was for a game show called *Guess My Secret*. She was talking to the camera, to him, daring him to discover her secret. The only clues she gave were a plate and a small clock. Soon she added a number of other clues into the mix—a pair of knitting needles and a jar of cocoa butter.

He was still scratching his head and laughing at her when she added more hints. Breath was sucked from his lungs when she placed two additional items on the table—a baby bottle and a bib. With a shaking hand, he reached over to turn up the volume while she smiled into the camera.

"Very good, Matthew. Since you're a smart man, I'm sure you now know my secret. We are having a baby! That's why I wanted to make our time here in Barcelona so special."

"Oh my God!" he groaned. Carmen had been pregnant? Then what happened?

"Hey, Matthew, I was beginning to think you got lost up here. What's going—"

Carmen entered the room and stopped talking in mid-sentence when she saw herself on the screen. Her gaze immediately sought out Matthew, and the pain she saw on his face tore at her heart.

"Is that true, Carmen? Had you planned to tell me that night in Barcelona that you were pregnant?"

She swallowed as she nodded. "Yes. I…I wanted to tell you in a fun way so…" Her words trailed off.

He nodded slowly and then asked the question she had been dreading. "What happened, Carmen?"

She lowered her head as she relived that night. The stomach pains that kept getting worse. Her not being able to reach him on his cell when she'd awakened that night, bleeding. Everything became a blur after that. Except the part about waking up and being told by a doctor that she'd lost the baby.

"Carmen?"

She lifted her head and met his gaze as her eyes filled with tears. And then she began speaking, recounting every single detail of that night. As she talked, she watched his expression. The shattered look on his face and the pain that clouded his eyes nearly broke her heart, and she felt his agony. A part of her was relieved to tell him the truth and no longer have the burden of keeping a secret on her shoulders.

"And you never told me," he said in a broken tone. "You never told me."

She pulled in a deep breath as tears threatened to spill down her face. "I couldn't. I wanted that baby so much. Losing it, and then not having you there with me to share my pain, made me bitter, unreasonable. I tried contacting you first and when I didn't get you, all I could think about was that I needed you and you were at work, away from me. In my emotional state, I blamed you."

He bent his head and when he raised his eyes to her again, the pain in them had deepened. "And I blame myself, as well," he said in a hoarse tone. "I blame myself because I should have been there with you. I don't know if I can ever forgive myself for not being there."

She saw the sheen of tears in his eyes and quickly crossed the room to him. As they clung to each other, tears she had held back since that night flowed down her face. She had cried then but it hadn't been like this. Her shoulders jerked with sobs she hadn't been able to let go of until now, until she was with him.

"I'm so sorry, Carmen. Now I understand. I had let you

down by letting you go through that alone. I know I won't ever be able to forgive myself for that."

She leaned away from him, wiping her eyes. "You can, Matthew, and you must. It took me a while to see it wasn't your fault, nor was it mine. The same thing would have happened if you'd been there. And being here with you this past week made me realize I can't be angry at you for something you didn't know about, something that was not in your control. I had tried telling you several times over the past week, but you kept wanting us to wait. I'm sorry you had to find out this way."

She wiped more tears from her eyes. "The woman who owned the villa called her doctor and made arrangements for him to take care of me there, figuring that I would want to keep it from the media. With her help, I was able to avoid the circus that could have taken place. The doctor said I can try again," she said, leaning up against him, holding tight. "But I so wanted that one," she whispered brokenly, burying her face in his chest.

Matthew swept her off her feet and carried her over to the settee. He sat down with her cradled in his lap. He bent his head, and felt his wet cheek against hers.

"It wasn't your fault, Matthew. It wasn't my fault. It was just something that happened. We have to believe that so we can move beyond it. There will be other babies."

He lifted his head to meet her gaze. "But will there be other babies…for us, Carmen? For you and me?"

Carmen knew what he was asking. He'd once told her that he didn't want any other woman to have his child but her. And from the look in his eyes he still wanted that. He wanted to know if their relationship would ever get back to the way it was, when he was her whole world and she was his.

She shifted slightly in his embrace to wrap her arms

around his neck. She wanted to make sure he heard what she was about to say. "I never stopped loving you, Matthew. The reason I wanted that baby so much was because it was a part of you, and a part of me. And the reason I hurt so much afterward was because I thought I had lost that connection. I thought the baby would bring us back together." She paused a second and then said, "But I've discovered that all it takes to bring us back together is us. Being with you here this past week has shown me there is still an us, and I want that back so badly. I was never involved with Bruno. It was all a publicity stunt. The only man I ever wanted to belong to was you. Can you forgive me for shutting you out of my life when I needed you most? Can you forgive me for running away? I will never leave you again."

"Oh, Carmen. I need you to forgive me, as well. I love you so much. I was so driven to give you the things you were used to having that I lost focus, I forgot about those things that truly mattered. You, and truly making you happy. I've been so lonely without you. And Candy, too, was just a publicity stunt. Hell, I was looking forward to spending time without her here. But when I arrived and discovered you, I wanted you to stay. At first I wanted revenge, to hurt you the way I was hurting, but I soon discovered it couldn't be that way with us."

She nodded. "I was going to make you want me and then leave again. Instead I ended up wanting you so badly I didn't know what to do."

"We're going to handle our business differently from here on out," he declared. "I've learned this week that I can balance my work and the rest of my life. Will you give me another chance to prove it?"

Carmen smiled up at him as he pushed back a strand of hair from her face. "I want that, too, Matthew."

"And will you marry me, Carmen?"

She felt more tears come to her eyes. "Yes, yes, I will marry you, and this time will be forever."

"Forever," he said, bending down to kiss her. And the kiss they shared was full of promise for a brighter and happier future. Together, knowing what they now knew about each other, they would be able to do anything.

Moments later he broke off the kiss and stood with her in his arms. She recognized the look he was giving her. "What about the polo match?" she asked.

He chuckled as he crossed the room to the bed. "There will be others."

Carmen knew he was right. Being in his arms and making love to him was what she needed. They were being given another chance at happiness and were taking it.

"It will be me and you together, Carmen, for the rest of our lives."

She reached up and caressed the side of his face. "Yes, Matthew, for the rest of our lives."

Epilogue

Ardella rushed over to them the moment Matthew and Carmen entered the tent, and from the anxious look on her face it was evident she was looking for a scoop. This time Matthew and Carmen didn't mind giving her one.

"So you two, what are you smiling about?"

Matthew pulled Carmen closer to his side. "It's a beautiful day and we believe it will be a good polo match."

The woman gave them a sly look. "I think there's something else."

Carmen decided to take Ardella out of her inquisitive misery. "There is something else and you can say you heard right from us. Matthew and I have decided to remarry."

The smile on the woman's face appeared genuine. "I truly happy for you two, but you know everyone will t details and facts."

armen threw her head back. "Sorry, but some things

we plan to keep secret and sacred." She refused to spill the beans about their plan to have a private ceremony on the beach here in the Hamptons this weekend. The first person she'd called was Rachel who had been supremely ecstatic.

"Matthew, will Carmen star in any future Birmingham movies?"

Matthew glanced down at Carmen and chuckled. "Ardella, Carmen can do anything Carmen wants."

Ardella beamed. "I will take that as a yes."

"You do that," Matthew said. And, knowing that Ardella probably had her secret camera ready, with the profound tenderness of a man who was in love, he pulled Carmen into his arms and kissed her.

No one would understand the emotions flowing through him at that that moment. They were the heartfelt emotions of a man meant to cherish the woman he loved. A man who'd recently realized that he really was husband material.

Carmen's heart was just as full and later, as she and Matthew sat beside each other watching the polo match, she couldn't help but wipe a tear from her eye. They had talked and together had promised not to let anything or anyone come between them again.

"You okay, sweetheart?"

Carmen glanced up at Matthew and nodded. "I couldn't be better." She paused and, still holding his gaze, whispered, "I love you."

A smile touched his lips. "And I love you."

She leaned closer to him when he tightened his arms around her shoulders. She was happy about the future that lay before them. He wanted to try again for a baby and so did she. But right now she looked forward to being Carmen Aiken Birmingham again.

She smiled, liking the sound of that and deciding to show him just how much when they returned home later. Life was good but being with the man you love, she decided, was even better.

* * * * *

THE SHEIKH'S
BARGAINED BRIDE

OLIVIA GATES

To the many fabulous ladies who made this novella
and this exciting miniseries come to life.
My senior editor, Krista Stroever, for the
wonderful premise and the unstinting guidance,
and authors Brenda Jackson, Yvonne Lindsay,
Catherine Mann, Katherine Garbera and Emily McKay
for all the fun and helpful collaboration.
It was a great experience working with you all.
I can't wait to do it again!

One

Three weeks ago, Sabrina Grant married the man of her dreams.

Sheikh Adham ben Khaleel ben Haamed Aal Ferjani was a prince—literally—who'd charmed and captivated her from the moment she'd set eyes on him. He was everything a woman couldn't be creative enough to hope for. She loved him with every fiber of her being.

And she'd never thought she could be so miserable.

How had she ended up like this? Alone, discarded? This was the last thing she'd imagined when she'd said "I do."

But then, she couldn't have imagined anything that had happened in the six weeks since her father's heart attack.

It had been late May, less than a week after she'd finished her postgraduate courses, and she'd been about to go home with two master's degrees in hand, when she'd been hit with the terrible news. She'd hurtled to his bedside, struggling with her anxiety as well as his, while fielding those who'd come to pay tribute to her father, Thomas Grant, multimillionaire vineyard and winery owner. The stress had almost wrecked her...until his best friend had come to visit, accompanied by the most incredible man she'd ever seen. Adham.

She was bowled over. And to her stunned delight, he seemed as taken with her. The best part was that she was sure his interest had nothing to do with her father's fortune. Beyond being second in line to the throne of the staggeringly rich desert kingdom of Khumayrah, he was the owner of the largest horse farm in the States, with a fortune that made her father's look like change.

Adham started coming every day, enthralling her more each time. He kept her company in her vigil at her father's bedside, took her for meals and walks. His companionship bolstered her while each touch inflamed her. By the time she begged for him and he took her, it was only three weeks into their relationship, but she'd already stumbled head over heels in love with him.

Then the next day, her father told her that he was being discharged, and that Adham had asked for her hand in marriage. She was overwhelmed by relief and happiness. Her father was going to be okay, and Adham loved her as much as she loved him.

But she crashed down to earth when she talked to her father's doctors. They said they were releasing him only because he'd asked to die at home. There was no use performing open-heart surgery, or even a heart transplant, since his other systems had been severely damaged, and he had only a few days to live.

Both her father and Adham agreed on an immediate wedding so that her father could witness it. She wanted to give him whatever happiness she could in his last days, but it was heart wrenching to know he wouldn't live to see her building a family with the man of her dreams.

Hours after the wedding, her father slipped into a coma. He died twenty-four hours later.

After such a tragic start to their marriage, it was the last thing she expected to have Adham whisk her away from her family home in Long Island, to deposit her in a mansion of his in New England and return to his obligations and duties. He came home only fleetingly, but certainly not to her.

She at first thought he was giving her time and space to mourn, so she tried to show him that she wanted nothing but to lose herself in his arms, that his intimacy would be the best salve for her grief.

When that didn't work, she looked everywhere for a reason for his withdrawal. She got a possible explanation when Jameel, his right-hand man who also supervised her *hashyah*—her entourage as a princess—told her there was a forty-day mourning period in Khumayrah, where normal life was interrupted to observe bereavement.

Now it was three weeks later, and she could no longer buy this. It was understandable to cancel their honeymoon in their situation, but to not come near her at all? To treat her like a stranger and not the bride she'd thought he hadn't been able to wait to possess again? That, she couldn't understand.

Just this morning, she'd again tried to speak to him. And again, he hadn't given her a chance.

He whisked her to the Hamptons for the start of the polo season, informing her of his many interests there. He was a player on one of the teams, as well as a patron who provided their horses, and a friend and associate to many of the pivotal people in the Bridgehampton Polo Club.

And here she was, in another one of his mansions, this

one even more impressive than the last—a spectacular estate on a dozen acres in a prime Bridgehampton South location, with a stunning floor plan, top-of-the-line building materials and masterful finishes. Its three floors covered thirty-six thousand square feet, and the grounds included a unique recreation pavilion. He'd said he liked to have his own residence when he came every year for the tournaments, and he needed all that space to accommodate his entourage and security.

He'd installed her in the master suite that boasted Bordeaux walnut floors, exquisite decor and an expansive en suite bathroom with gold fixtures and onyx walls and floors. The only thing it didn't include was her groom.

"Sabrina."

She jerked out of her morbid musings. *Adham*.

His voice had come from the suite's sitting-room door. Fathomless, irresistible, the exotic inflections of his native Khumayran that mixed with his upper-crust British accent turning her name into an invocation.

In spite of the crushed expectations and confusion of the past weeks, hope surged, making her dizzy with it.

Maybe he would come to her at last. Maybe he *had* withdrawn to give her time to mourn her father, and had postponed their wedding night until he was sure she was up to withstanding his passion.

If that was it, she'd thank him for his consideration and adherence to his culture's mourning rituals, then scold him for not understanding the last thing she needed was to feel cut off with her grief. She didn't need space and time. She needed *him*.

Her breath caught in her lungs as she leaned back on the king-size, white-lace-covered bed. He'd walk in any second now.

Seconds stretched. Then she heard his receding foot-steps.

She sat up, stunned. He'd called only so she'd come out, and walked away when she hadn't, rather than be in a bedroom with her? Why?

Then you *call* him, *you moron. Find out why. Once and for all.*

"Adham."

But she was too late. The door clicked closed behind him.

And she couldn't take it anymore. She exploded from the bed, running after him.

She called out again as she pursued him. But even though he must have heard her, he strode ahead undeterred.

This time, so would she. She had to get to the bottom of this or lose her mind.

She ran after him through the maze of a dazzling parterre, her heels grinding the gravel paths. She caught up with him before he lowered himself into the driver's seat of a gleaming black Jaguar that seemed like an extension of him, of his power and potency.

He turned to her, his eyes hidden behind mirrored sunglasses, his face blank. God. She missed his smile.

"Sabrina." That revving *R,* underlining his exotic origins, shuddered through her again. "I thought you were asleep."

"I'd be narcoleptic if I were asleep every time you think I am."

He didn't smile. Probably because of the bitterness that had stained her tone.

He looked down the eight inches between them—even with her three-inch heels—the wealth of his rain-straight hair gleaming like a raven's wing in the midday summer sun. She almost moaned as everything about him bombarded her. His scent, his size, his beauty. He'd changed out of the casual clothes he'd worn while piloting the helicopter out to the Hamptons into one of those designer suits that made him look almost intimidating. At thirty-four, he was the epitome of everything male, of what she'd never imagined could be gathered in one man. And he was her husband. Yet he wasn't really hers at all.

Suddenly, all thoughts, all existence disappeared.

Adham was taking off his sunglasses, his golden eyes flaring with their emerald highlights, reaching out a hand to cup her face in a possessive palm. His thumb stroked her cheek, skimmed over her trembling lips, dipping into their moistness, spreading it over them, setting everything he touched on fire.

"You look edible, *ya jameelati.*"

Hearing him call her "my beauty," and the way he was gazing at her as if he did want to devour her, thundered through her.

Her response was so fierce, it sent indignation rippling through her. "I look exactly the same as I did this morning. I haven't even changed out of my traveling clothes."

"Then I beg your forgiveness for not noticing. I had too many urgencies on my mind. But that's no excuse. Nothing should have distracted me from *kanzi, aroosi*—my treasure, my bride."

Before she could process his words, or register the surge of joy they elicited, his hand slid to her nape, holding her head captive, the other gathering her around her waist and lifting her off the ground, plastering her against his steel-fleshed body.

"Adham…" was all she gasped before his lips took hers.

He drank her moans, thrusting his tongue inside her, occupying her, intoxicating her. "*Aih, gooly esmi haik*—say my name like that, like you can't draw breath with wanting me."

"I can't...." She writhed in his arms, not caring that they were out in the open. She'd starved for him.

He turned, pressing her against the back passenger door, thrust against her, his daunting erection digging into her quivering stomach, his knee driving between her melting thighs.

One thing was left inside her mind, looping in a frenzied litany. *He wants me again.*

"I would say get a room, but we're standing in front of a mansion with sixteen suites. And by the look of it, you've probably made thorough use of each and every one of them."

The words, spoken by a deep, amused male voice, trickled through Sabrina's fevered awareness. She only understood that Adham was severing their meld and putting her back fully on her feet. She clung to him, panicked he'd drift away again.

But he brought her in front of him as he turned to the speaker, his arms gathering her tight, linking over her belly.

She blinked through the crimson haze of arousal at a tall, dark, handsome man standing a dozen feet away, his hands deep in the pockets of his ultra-chic pants. He looked highly entertained.

"And hello to you, too, Seb." Adham's voice above her ear had more moist heat surging between her thighs. She struggled not to rub them together, to ameliorate the pounding there. "It's great that you came, *ya sudeeki,* so I can have the pleasure—" his hands brushed her belly with insistent caresses, his hardness jerking against the small of her back "—of introducing to you the love of my life, my bride, Sabrina Aal Ferjani." Sabrina didn't know how she remained upright after such a declaration. "*Ameerati,* let me introduce Sebastian Hughes, my friend and associate. He runs the Bridgehampton Polo Club in his father's stead."

She extended a trembling hand to Sebastian, over-whelmed at Adham calling her "my princess" on top of everything else.

Sebastian placed a gallant kiss on her hand. "It's an honor and a pleasure to meet you, Sabrina." He raised green eyes full of mischief, before he straightened to a height a couple of inches shy of Adham's six foot five. "And a shock. I never thought the day would come when Adham entered matrimony's gilded cage willingly."

"I never thought it would, either." Adham looked down, his gaze singeing her. "Until I met Sabrina. And then nothing could have kept me out of it. Not that anywhere she is could be called a cage, gilded or otherwise, but a haven."

Sebastian barked a laugh. "Oh, man. You're spouting poetry! You must have potent magic, Sabrina. I can call you Sabrina, right?" Before she could blurt out an affirmation, Sebastian turned his teasing eyes to Adham. "You won't make me call her Princess Aal Ferjani, will you, Adham?"

Adham's smile flashed, riddling her vision in spots. "He's having a field day teasing me, since just before I met you, I told him that he'd never see me married. But then I can say the same about him. While we were falling in love, the world's foremost confirmed bachelor had a change of heart, too. It took his assistant almost leaving him to make him realize he can't live without her."

Sebastian nodded whimsically. "Yeah. One thing for sure, Sabrina, Adham and I are both lucky dogs. And you and Julia must be saints for not only putting up with us, but for forgiving our trespasses and loving us nevertheless."

"Why do you think Adham had any trespasses to forgive?" The question was out of her mouth before she could think.

Sebastian's lips twisted whimsically. "Because as an inveterate lone wolf, he must have committed some in his struggles not to succumb to his fate and his feelings for you. I know I did."

Suddenly it felt like floodlights went on inside her head.

Could that be what the past weeks were about? Adham trying to adjust to being married, after a lifetime of thinking he'd never tie his life to another?

"So what brings you here, Seb?" Adham asked, interrupting her musings. "I was just coming to the farm myself."

"I thought you wouldn't make it out on Sabrina's first day here, so I came to meet your bride and welcome her to our neck of the woods."

"And now you have." Adham turned his eyes to her. "And now that you're here, would you like to accompany me, *ya ameerati?* I'd love to give you a tour of the Seven Oaks Farm, where the polo club's tournaments take place."

She almost jumped in his arms. "Oh, yes, please."

Sebastian laughed. "And in case things get too hot for you during the tour, you can borrow my personal quarters at the farm to…cool off."

Adham shook his head. "Suffering in utmost discomfort doesn't matter, when one's waiting for the time to be finally right."

She twisted to gaze into his eyes, and saw it again. The pure, unadulterated passion of the life-changing night when he'd possessed her.

He meant those words. He had been waiting for her to heal, the incredible—if terribly misguided—man.

And she felt her life begin. Finally. For real.

TWO

The drive to the Seven Oaks Farm passed in a haze.

All Sabrina felt was Adham sitting beside her, his body radiating command and control, all she saw was his sculpted profile, all she could appreciate was his profound beauty. The man was gorgeous down to his last hair and pore.

And all she wanted was to carry on where they'd left off when Sebastian had interrupted them. She'd thought he'd intended to when he'd decided to have Jameel chauffeur them in a limo. But with the barrier between driver and passenger compartments down, and his bodyguards preceding and following them in other cars, she felt exposed. And then, even if she didn't, she wouldn't have acted on the desires churning in her mind, frying her body.

She wouldn't have run her hand up his inner thigh, wouldn't have leaned over him to rub his hardness with her leg and catch his maddening lower lip in her teeth. She had to face it. She was too inexperienced; she'd probably botch any seduction attempt. Worse, she was too shy to try, even if she was assured of the desired results. She still needed him to initiate their intimacies.

No such luck. He'd been inundated with one phone call after another since they'd entered the limo. She could only watch him, vibrating with his nearness, with ratcheting need.

"*Zain, kaffa*. That's enough," he growled under his breath as he ended the last call. "I'm turning the phone off. They'll have to live without me for a while." He turned to her. "*Aassef, ya habibati*. So sorry for all this. There will be no more interruptions. So tell me. What do you know about polo?"

Heat rushed to her face at hearing him calling her "my love." She'd memorized everything he'd said to her in his native tongue and investigated what it meant when he hadn't provided the translation. He'd called her that only once before—when he'd been deep in her, turning her inside out with pleasure.

She mumbled her answer. "Uh...not much."

"Let me guess. A group of men galloping on horses, hitting a tiny ball around a huge field with sticks to catapult it between goal posts." Her heat rose another notch in embarrassment. That was exactly how it seemed to her. The amused indulgence in his eyes poured fuel on her conflagration. "And you wouldn't be wrong. That's basically it. Want to know more about the sport and the events I'm going to be involved in for the next few weeks?"

"Please." Her heart kicked with eagerness to know more of what he enjoyed, what made up his passions and occupations. "Tell me everything."

Something she couldn't define came into in his eyes. He looked away for a moment, catching Jameel's eyes in the front mirror. Before she could wonder, his eyes were back, snaring hers, wiping her mind clean of anything but her yearning for him.

"I started playing polo when I was eight." Her heart melted inside her rib cage at imagining him at that age, the most beautiful boy, the strongest and smartest, already such an accomplished rider that he could excel in the fierce sport. "And I started breeding my own horses at sixteen. For the past ten years, I've played an integral role in every major polo tournament in the world, as sponsor, horse supplier and player. But I have a special interest in the one that takes place here every summer, especially since Sebastian took over after his father was diagnosed with cancer. For the past three weeks I've been commuting here for the preseason tournament, The Clearwater Media Cup, a run-up to the main season. Clearwater Media is the company Sebastian owns with Richard Wells, who's just become engaged to one of my best horse trainers, Catherine Lawson. Their engagement almost coincided with Sebastian's to his assistant, Julia."

She wanted to blurt out, "And with our marriage." But she hesitated, because it didn't feel real yet. She only said, "And the season hasn't even started yet."

"This summer's tournament *is* going to be memorable. It's always high stakes with the world's best athletes competing for one of the sport's most treasured prizes amid the splendor of the Hamptons summer scene." He suddenly cupped her face. "But this year it will be the best ever because you're here. With me."

She almost fainted with the surge of emotions as she gazed helplessly into the molten translucence of his eyes.

A scratchy noise came from what felt like a mile away. She didn't realize what it was until Adham withdrew his hand and sat back. Jameel's discreet cough, alerting them that they'd arrived.

She looked dazedly around. They'd stopped by a row of stables. There were people outside. Some seemed to be going about their business. Most seemed to be waiting for them. With cameras.

She turned to Adham, apprehension shooting up her spine. She didn't find him. Seconds later, he seemed to materialize at her other side. He helped her out and she stumbled up and into his containment as the glare and heat of the summer day and the cacophony of the newspeople bombarded her. He hugged her to his side as they walked inside the stables, preceded by rabidly eager faces, snapping photos and shouting questions.

Adham calmly confirmed the date of their marriage, and that it had been a private ceremony because of her father's condition. Then he nodded to Jameel, and bodyguards appeared as if out of nowhere, clearing their path of paparazzi.

There were still too many people inside the stables, too many eyes, all on Adham and her. She felt more vulnerable by the second under their scrutiny. She'd always hated attention. She'd realized she'd get more than ever now that she was Adham's wife, but realizing it was one thing. Experiencing it was another.

A tremor shot through her. Adham's arm tightened, making her feel he'd surrounded her with a protective force field, as if she were the most treasured thing on earth.

"I want you to meet my most important colleagues."

Next second, all unease evaporated. It was replaced by wonder.

His horses. Or as they were called in polo, his ponies.

The sight of the mind-boggling collection of magnificent

animals had delight bubbling inside her at being so close to such a manifestation of primal grandeur and beauty.

Adham introduced her to each pony, telling her its name, breed, measurements, character, quirks and strengths on the field. And throughout, people came to salute him, awe for him as clear as their curiosity about her, the woman this desert prince and celebrity entrepreneur had picked to be his bride.

He accepted their congratulations, deflected their adulation and introduced her with supreme pride, then made it clear that he expected privacy to show his bride around.

Once everyone had retreated to an acceptable distance, Adham resumed his explanations. "My ponies travel with me wherever my team goes. Each member must have six to eight horses per game. But to make allowances for injuries and other crises, I transport around sixty to seventy horses during each season."

Just when she thought she couldn't possibly see anything more perfect, he introduced her to his pride and joy, his prize ponies.

"Aswad and Layl, 'black' and 'night' in Arabic, are brothers. Their sire was Hallek, or 'deepest dark,' my very first horse."

She caressed one glossy velvet neck after another in wonder, flashing Adham a delighted smile. "Any relation, since your own name means 'deepest black'?"

He let out a peal of laughter that had every head in the stables turning, relinquishing any attempt to appear as if they weren't intently watching their every move.

"My family always wondered if I have horse genes in me, the way I'm as one with them. But it's true that I feel like they're my kin, my children even. I oversaw the breeding of each and every one of my ponies myself, followed their lives since before they were born."

"You do share all of their unrivaled magnificence."

At her fervent statement, his eyes flared. He plunged his fingers into the mass of curls at the back of her head, cupped her neck in his large palm as he crowded her against Aswad. "It's your magnificence that can't be rivaled, *ya jameelati.*"

At the periphery of her fogging awareness, she heard a whirring sound. It was only when Adham removed his hand and shifted his eyes to the source of disturbance that she realized what it had been. One of the paparazzi had managed to slip by the bodyguards.

Adham glared at him. The guy only grinned, taking more photos. Adham advanced on him and the thin, seedy-looking guy clambered back out of the stables.

Sabrina put her hand on Adham's clenched forearm. "Aswad and Layl are Arabian?"

He looked back at her, the knowledge that she was trying to defuse the situation filling his eyes.

He let her have her wish, visibly relaxed, smiled. "All my ponies are purebred Arabian stallions and mares. You can tell by this." He ran his hand lovingly down Layl's head. The horse nuzzled him back in delight and affection. She knew exactly how he felt. "A refined, wedge-shaped head." He grabbed her closer, pressing his length to her back, running his hands down her arms until he entwined their fingers before he raised her hands so they could caress each feature of Layl he mentioned.

"They also have a broad forehead, large eyes and nostrils, small muzzles, an arched neck and a high tail carriage. Most have a slight forehead bulge, what we call *jibbah* in Khumayrah." He guided her fingertips in investigating the protrusion. "It's an enlargement of their sinuses that helps them weather our desert climate. And with compact bodies and short backs, even small Arabians can carry heavy riders with ease. They're known for stamina and courage. But I've never known a horse with half of Aswad's and Layl's endurance and fearlessness. I ride them in games at critical times. They play to win."

By now she was feeling he'd explored every inch of *her* body. Then he made it even worse, turned her to him. "The season's tournaments are played on six consecutive Saturdays and proceeds benefit charities. A match lasts about two hours, divided into six 'chukkers,' seven minutes each. During half time, spectators indulge in the social tradition of divot stomping, or evening out the ground for the players."

His informative discourse clashed with the hunger in his eyes, the coveting in his touch. Her state was only ameliorated when he gave her space to breathe, to play with the horses.

Then he hugged her off the ground, pressing his lips to her neck. "How about we meet my biped friends now?"

She twisted around and looked up at him. The solitary dimple in his cheek had her heart revving like a car with its accelerator pedal floored.

"Only if you promise I can see your ponies again." She sounded as if she'd been running a mile.

"I promise you anything you want, whenever you want it." She wanted to cry out that she wanted only one thing— him. "Everyone must be at the VIP tent, and I'm certain they can't wait to meet you. They're a great group of people. My friends are, anyway. These tournaments are celebrity populated, and they can be a magnet for all kinds."

She nodded. She knew only too well what kind of people were attracted to fame and fortune.

He hugged her to his side again, leading her out to the tent.

She searched for something to say. Preferably something intelligent this time. She'd been a swooning idiot in his arms so far, and a giddy child with his horses. "So, what makes a good polo player?"

His eyes crinkled with pleasure at her attempt to engage him. "The ability to ride like a desert raider, to hit the ball like a medieval knight and to work the game like a champion chess player all while someone is trying to beat your knees off."

"Yikes!" He threw his head back at her alarm, letting out a guffaw of sheer amusement. She leaned deeper into his body, delighting in having his large, solid form pressing against her again. "Have you ever been injured?"

"Injuries are part of such an intense contact sport where the competition has always been dubbed 'bruising.'"

Her heart pounded. "But that's it, right? The worst of it is bruises?"

His eyes stilled on hers. With doubt? Disbelief?

Next second she saw nothing in them but indulgence. She must have imagined what she'd thought she'd seen. "The more experienced a player is, the fewer injuries he'll have. Sometimes everyone gets away with nothing, sometimes with a few bruises, but there's always the possibility of a more lasting souvenir. Injuries throughout polo history ranged from lacerations to fractures to brain injury to death. The worst injuries happen if a saddle breaks, or ponies collide at top speed, or someone gets thrown off."

"Oh, God." Her stomach squeezed into her throat as she imagined him sustaining an injury—or worse.

Her heart contracted violently with the need to beg him to never play again. But she couldn't voice her plea. She didn't feel like his wife for real yet. Not that she believed spouses could interfere in each other's passions anyway. And then she was certain he was careful, in control of his game.

But what if...?

She couldn't bear it. She had to articulate her dread, to make sense of it all. "But if there are such risks, why play?"

He shrugged. "Life is filled with risks. People who are totally safe are already dead."

"But you're super careful, right? No saddles of yours can break, and you always watch out for rabid antagonists?"

Again his eyes took on that enigmatic cast. "If you're asking if I'm a risk taker, I'm anything but. I'm a planner. A strategist. I set a goal, put everything in motion and invariably see my plans through to fruition." Suddenly an edge of harshness flashed in his gaze as he added, "But then, so do you."

Three

Sabrina stared at Adham, a frisson of unease slithering in her gut. The way he'd said that…

She had a feeling he meant something beyond polo playing.

Which only figured. He was a businessman, who played the real estate and horse-breeding worlds like a virtuoso.

But what did he mean, so did she? Did he mean that she'd let nothing stop her from acquiring the degrees she needed to take her place beside her father in their family business? Yes, that must be it. And the hardness she'd imagined accompanied his words must have been a trick of her still-agitated mind. Now settled on this front, her mind swung back to her main concern. "So you've never been injured?"

"I didn't say that. You remember that scar on my thigh?"

She'd never forget. She'd been horrified to see it. She'd

touched it in trepidation, the pain he must have felt on sustaining it echoing inside her.

"That was my most severe injury. My pony fell on top of my leg. My femur fractured and ripped through my thigh."

She felt darkness encroaching on her as she imagined his flesh being torn, his blood pouring out. Her fingers dug into his arm, as if she could pull him away from hurt and injury, give him her own vitality to heal any pain he'd ever suffered.

He pressed her tighter against him, accepting her concern, paying her back in sheer mind-numbing sensuality. "But you made me glad I have this scar."

She felt blood rushing to her head, pooling in her loins as she remembered how she'd traced it. He'd sprawled back, letting her explore it, stroking her in turn. She couldn't help it, had opened her mouth over it, sucked at its ridges as if she could smooth them out.

And she'd gotten her first look at what he was like aroused. She'd been too shy so far to do more than open herself to him, take him inside her body, not daring to look at the huge hardness that had invaded her, had her sobbing in an excruciating mixture of pain and pleasure. Her head had spun at the sight of him. Then she'd been compelled to explore his daunting beauty. She'd quaked with his feral rumbles at her ministrations. Then he'd taken her over, given her the hard ride she'd been disintegrating for.

She was suffering from the same need now. But first she had to suffer more deprivation, be his bride to the polo community, make him proud. They'd arrived at the VIP tent.

At their entry there was an uproar of welcomes and congratulations, with more camera flashes from sanctioned celebrity reporters, and many of the guests.

She'd thought she was ready but she found herself wishing that floors really opened and swallowed people. And she'd thought she'd known social attention as Thomas Grant's daughter. She'd known nothing. Now she was Sheikh Adham Aal Ferjani's bride, she had a feeling this was just the tip of the iceberg.

The next thirty minutes was a maelstrom of introductions to hordes of beautiful and high profile people. She tried her best to be as gracious as Adham in accepting the tribute everyone was paying her as the bride of their most valued guest and invaluable sponsor. She had a feeling she was doing a miserable job.

Most of the women around gobbled him up with their eyes. Many ignored her, making blatant offers of availability. It was only because Adham looked at them as he would bales of hay that Sabrina's chagrin was held at bay. And then she realized she'd better get used to it. After all, what woman could be around Adham and not lose all control?

It was only when Adham took her to meet his core group of friends and associates that her mood improved.

There was Sebastian and his fiancée, Julia Fitzgerald, with Sebastian's partner, Richard Wells, and his fiancée Catherine Lawson, Adham's horse trainer. They were accompanied by Nicolas Valera, a renowned Argentinean polo player and model who played on Adham's team, the Black Wolves.

After a stretch of small talk, Julia said, "Tell us about your vineyards and winery, Sabrina. I'm ashamed to say I didn't even know that Long Island had vineyards."

"Many people don't know. My father was among the first to realize that the microclimate here was similar to that found in Bordeaux. He released his first wines in 1975. During the last three decades, the Long Island wine industry has expanded—today there are dozens of vineyards planted on thousands of acres. The vines yield high quality grapes similar to those used by the French and Californian winemakers. Grant Vineyards produces world-class merlot, cabernet franc, cabernet sauvignon and chardonnay."

"Wow!" Catherine exclaimed. "You sure know your business. Did you start working with your father when you were young?"

A vise clamped Sabrina's heart as she remembered her frustration at her father's misguided overprotection. "Actually, he didn't want me to, but I insisted on learning everything about the vineyards and winery. I have master's degrees in business and administration, *and* brewing and winemaking. I was determined to help him run the business, and take over for him when he decided to retire. But he didn't get the chance to...."

Her words faltered as her eyes filled with tears. Julia and Catherine reached out to her, empathy etching their faces. Sabrina felt solace pouring from them but it was Adham's tightening hold that eased the anguish.

Responding to Adham's subtle prompt, Nicolas changed the topic, engaging Adham in a verbal game as exhilarating and bruising as any of their polo matches, which had the ladies dissolving in laughter. Seeing the intention behind Adham's maneuver, Sabrina felt herself stumbling deeper in love with him.

But though she enjoyed his friends' company, after an hour, the need to get away rose. She needed to be with him, alone, to settle her mind about their situation.

She was trying to figure out how to let him know that without sounding like a clingy, demanding wife, when he again seemed to sense her need. He suavely thanked his friends on her behalf for their fabulous welcome, and slipped her away.

He took her to the far end of the tent, and she blurted out the first thing that came to her, unable to say what she truly wanted to say. "So, you told me what makes a good polo player. What makes a great one?"

He looked at her for a second, then said, "Apart from having thoroughly trained ponies, and an ability to read them, it's focus."

"If that's what it takes, I bet you're the greatest."

He smiled down at her, clearly amused by her adulation, and—pleased, too? Even touched? "I don't know about *the* greatest. But I am one of the few who've been ranked at a ten-goal handicap."

"What does that mean?"

"Polo players are rated yearly by their peers on a scale of two to ten goals. The term 'goal' doesn't refer to how many goals the player will score in a match, but indicates the player's value to the team. Player handicaps range from novice—or negative two—to ten, which is perfect. A rating of above two goals indicates a professional player."

"And you're, of course, perfect. But I already knew that."

He put a finger under her chin and tilted her head up. His gaze blazed down on her for a long moment as he seemed to vibrate with something vast and uncontainable, sweeping her in a swath of lust that singed her down to her bones. Then he kissed her. She pressed against him, her head falling back, sending her heavy curls cascading over his arm as it clutched her waist.

When he relinquished her lips in agonizing slowness, he left her panting for more. The ferocious appreciation in his eyes made her feel intoxicated, brazen.

"So that's your handicap," she whispered, her voice husky with arousal. "What's your preferred…position?"

At her barely veiled innuendo, his pupils engulfed the gold of his eyes like a black hole would the sun. "Any and every position. As long as it fulfills the purpose of the… game." She shuddered with the need eating through her, to have him pleasure her in all those positions. She'd been going crazy reliving the memories of the times they'd been together. "But my preferred position is number three."

For a moment she thought he meant the third time he'd taken her, that next morning, when he'd had her riding him as he'd suckled her nipples and fondled her triggers. He went on, a devilish smile on his masterpiece lips. "It's similar to a quarterback in football, usually reserved for the highest handicapped and most experienced player. It entails attacking the opposing offense and turning the ball up field, requiring long-distance hitting accuracy and superb mallet and ball control."

"And we all know what kind of control you have." She actually meant his ability to stay away from her, but he clearly thought she meant his control during lovemaking. His gaze smoldered until she felt he was burning her up from the inside out. Unable to deal with the unease and embarrassment of explaining her true meaning, she reverted to her earlier worry. "So, after your injury, didn't you hesitate before getting back on a horse, embroiled in another bruising polo match?"

"Not for a second. There's nothing more exhilarating than going at a speed of thirty-five miles an hour on a horse you feel as one with. It's such a pleasure and privilege to form a bond and share the synergy of the play with a horse. And then there is the breeze rushing against your face as time stands still while you swing the mallet knowing the exact second you'll hit the ball, feeling the satisfaction of catapulting it exactly where you want it, setting up the play that will end up in a score."

She sighed. "You make me wish I played polo."

"If you so wish it, then so shall it be."

She shook her head wistfully. "I can't even ride a horse. My father never let me. At first he said I was too young, too slight. Then after my mom died, he became even more overprotective. I had to fight for each inch of independence, and riding horses was one of the things I decided to forgo in order to have other things. He even made me swear I'd never ride while I was away at college. I always felt so... deprived. I contented myself with taking every opportunity to visit with our vineyards' horses."

"I can tell you love horses. Aswad and Layl took to you immediately. I'm sure they'd love to have your company whenever possible."

She sighed again. "But now that you've outlined the real dangers of riding, I can better understand my father's worry."

Something strange came into Adham's eyes again. What was this? Was he angry? At whom? Her father, for limiting her? Or at himself for planting in her mind worry over his beloved sport?

Next second, the ominous cloud disappeared and the world was bright and shining once more. He bent to press the warmth of his magical lips on her pulse. It went haywire. "Don't worry, *ya galbi*. Not about me."

"I couldn't bear it if anything happened to you. Please, be careful."

He pressed her closer. "I always am. But I now have more reason than ever to be so."

She felt her consciousness receding. She was *swooning,* like a heroine from a Victorian novel. Before she'd met Adham, she'd suspected she might be really frigid, as many men had accused her. If those small-minded, vicious men could see her now.

A discreet cough came from behind Adham. Jameel.

Adham half turned to him. Their exchange in Arabic was rapid. She didn't get one word. Then he turned to her, his lids still heavy with desire but with an apology on his lips. "I'm sorry, *ya ameerati*. Urgent business has come up. Please stay, mingle some more. Jameel will drive you home when you're ready."

Disappointment spread through her but she smiled at him. "Oh, no. You attend your business and I'll go home now. I'll…I'll wait for you."

"As you wish." He swept her around and walked her out of the tent, nodding to everyone who seemed more curious than before, if possible. She'd sure given them a spectacle worthy of curiosity. The blushing bride who now had plenty to blush about.

Thirty minutes later, she was back in the Hamptons residence. She had no idea how long his business would take, but she rushed to get ready for his return.

An hour later, she'd bathed and dressed in what she hoped was an irresistible creation.

Two hours later, she called him. His phone went straight to voice mail. She didn't leave a message.

What was going on? Where was he? What could possibly keep him away after the enchanted day they'd shared?

She tried to tell herself that she'd married a businessman and a man of state, and that his time wasn't his to control.

It didn't work. While all that was true, a simple call would have allowed her to go to sleep knowing that their marriage was not a mirage that could appear and disappear at his whim. His reverting to the man who didn't bother to tell her where he was or what he was doing tossed her back into her former state of turmoil.

The last thing she knew before she succumbed to exhaustion was that Adham hadn't come home.

Her nightmares throughout the night said he never would.

Four

She woke up alone. As she had all her life.

The first thing that came to her was a conviction: that she'd wake up alone for the rest of it, too.

She'd also gone to bed alone. As she had since she'd married Adham.

She'd thought after that first day in the Hamptons that the inexplicable hands-off phase had passed.

It hadn't. The past week had followed the same pattern. He'd be all over her during the day, then would disappear at night, every time with one excuse or another.

She dragged herself out of bed. She felt as if the silky sheets and downy covers were spread with thorns.

The room was swathed in cool, dark silence. She knew out there another day blazed with heat and light, bustling with the sounds of Adham's housekeepers tirelessly keeping this place immaculate. Blackout blinds and soundproof doors and windows shielded her from it all. The room echoed with isolation. Inertia.

She felt as if she'd been on a roller coaster without a harness, one that catapulted her up, made her feel she was soaring, only to crash her to the ground, leaving her stunned and crushed, only to start all over again.

If it weren't for that one night, when he'd proved he was as over-endowed sexually as he was in every other way, she'd have thought his lack of interest in intimacy stemmed from some deficiency. But since his potency was indisputable, she'd feared he'd somehow lost interest in *her*. Yet over the past week, he'd showed her proof, physical and verbal, of his need to possess her. But he'd left her alone again, every night, and now she feared he might be accepting those women's offers.

She couldn't really believe that, but she'd run out of excuses for his behavior. Not wanting to rush her after her bereavement no longer made sense. Preoccupation didn't hold water, either.

What kind of game was he playing?

Her cell phone rang. She stared at it numbly before she realized it was the special tone she'd assigned to Adham.

She pounced on it, sending it flying off her night-stand.

By the time she answered, she was panting. Air crammed in her lungs when his dark voice poured into her ear.

"Sabah'al khair, ya galbi."

Just hearing him say good morning in his mother tongue would have been enough. Hearing him say anything. But when he called her *his heart,* in that intimate, possessive way...

Before she could cry out her confusion, he went on, "I hope you've had some...rest."

The way he paused before he said *rest*. He thought she

was so distraught, she couldn't rest even when she managed to fall asleep?

No. There was satisfaction, not concern, in his voice. As if he liked the reason she needed rest. Anyone hearing him would assume he'd been that reason, after he'd tested her stamina in an exhausting session of passion and possession.

More confused than ever, she breathed, "I slept. Sort of. I—I missed you."

"And I more than missed you, *ya kanzi*. But I have to be here the whole day. I have back-to-back practice sessions. If you're up to it, Jameel will drive you over. You can watch me practice, or you can mingle with the ladies. You don't have to stay long."

"I want to watch you. I'll stay as long as you do, and go home with you."

"Then—come."

The way he said that—her nipples stung, her core clenched.

And suddenly, she was angry. Enraged.

She felt like a mouse after a capricious feline had taken turns licking and petting it, then knocking it around. She felt battered and desperate.

And she'd had enough.

"On second thought, I won't."

There was a prolonged silence on his end after her sudden change of tone. She could feel tension mushrooming through the ether, sending its electrifying tentacles into her body.

But when he spoke again, his voice betrayed no surprise or irritation. "I thought so, *ya ameerati*." His voice dipped into its darkest reaches, like it had only once before when he'd been driving inside her, scalding her with growls of praise and pleasure. "Do get all the rest you can. You'll need it."

Then he ended the call.

She felt she'd explode with frustration. She quaked with the force of it, with the urge to storm to the farm, grab and shake him, scream at him, demanding an explanation for his tormenting behavior.

Then the seizure passed. The calm of resolution slowly descended.

She'd take his advice. She'd get all the rest she could. She *was* going to need it. For the showdown she'd have with him.

She'd have this out with him, even if it was the last straw that would break their marriage. Their non-marriage.

Anything was better than this limbo.

She didn't rest.

Adham must have known she wouldn't. Couldn't.

Not that he cared. He'd come home very late and disappeared somewhere. As usual.

At eight in the morning, she'd been sitting in the grand foyer for two hours, waiting for him to make an appearance. She would intercept him before he pulled another disappearing act.

Then she heard his steps. Her heart clanged in her chest as he approached. Then its beats scattered as they receded. He'd made a detour, entered his study.

She rose on quivering legs. Her breath jammed in her chest as she approached it. She felt as if she was nearing a landmine.

She grilled herself over her stupidity and weakness.

Just get it over with. Once and for all.

She ground her teeth as she turned the handle. Then with one last bolstering gulp of oxygen, she walked in.

She knew he felt her come in, but he didn't raise his eyes from the dossier he had open before him on his hand-carved, polished mahogany desk.

Well, she was damned if she'd let him ignore her again and continue playing this sadistic game with her.

This ended now.

"Adham."

It took him several nerve-fraying seconds to raise his eyes at her curtness, his face a study in blankness.

There he was again. The remote stranger he reverted to when they were alone. She suddenly realized they had only been alone for minutes since their wedding. Someone else had almost always been around.

So what was it with the Jekyll-and-Hyde reaction to privacy? Had it been triggered by their wedding ceremony? He sure hadn't suffered from this affliction before it.

"I'm busy, Sabrina." His voice was as expressionless as his face. "This can wait."

Her outrage crested. "No, this can't wait. You're not putting me off again."

He put down his pen, adjusting his pose to that of someone bent on suffering a pest's interruption with utmost forbearance. "When have I put you off in the first place?"

"Oh, boy." She huffed a chuckle fueled by all her fury and frustration. "You are a piece of work."

"I fail to grasp your meaning. It must be a breakdown in communication, originating from our different grasps on the nuances of language."

"Don't play the 'cultural difference' card. You were educated in the West, and you've lived here for big chunks of time since childhood. The only one who has a problem understanding anything is me. But now you're going to explain. Start by enlightening me about your view of marriage, since it seems it doesn't coincide with mine."

The stillness in his body seemed to deepen. "And what is your view of marriage?"

"That of almost everyone on the planet, in any culture. A man and a woman who actually live together."

"I live with you."

"You mean you grace whichever residence you happen to install me in with your fleeting presence."

He gave a slight shrug of one formidable shoulder. "To the world, I do live with you. I come home to you every night."

"What does the world matter here? *I* know you don't. And I demand to know what you're playing at."

His body seemed to harden to rock, his face becoming almost inanimate. "I don't appreciate your tone."

A frisson of danger arced through her but she ignored it. He could think again if he thought she would be daunted by his dismissal or displeasure. "Well, tough. This is the only tone you're getting since you refuse to acknowledge my questions. I won't be brushed aside again until you suddenly remember I'm supposed to be your wife. Only in public, of course."

His gaze became arctic. Then his baritone drenched her with its pitiless coldness. "If you're worried this indicates I'm thinking of reneging on our deal, put your mind to rest."

She dazedly stared at him. "Our deal?"

"Is still in effect. You have no reason to fear I won't keep my end of the bargain. My father's edict remains unchanged, and I still need an heir. You know that I already settled your father's debts, securing the Grant name. And I will, in due course, secure your future." His gaze panned downward, obscuring his expression, before he looked back up, impaling her on icicles. "But I now realize the source of your anxiety. It seems your father, either due to his rapid deterioration, or because he thought that you knew enough, didn't inform you of the specifics of the deal he negotiated on your behalf."

His father's edict. An heir. Her father's debts. The Grant name. Her future. It all made no sense.

She heard her own hoarse rasp. "What specifics?"

He rose from his seat. The room felt as if it were shrinking, as if its walls were closing in on her. "As per the contracts I signed, I'll run the winery and vineyards until you conceive, then I'll give you back their rights. When you carry my child to term, I'll give you the capital and the experts you need to run them. I'll keep the two hundred acres your father never got around to planting. But since *my* father's terms specified that my wife must be pregnant a year after the wedding, and since I've already consummated our relationship, I can afford to wait to see if you are already pregnant. In a couple of weeks, if you aren't, I'll take you to bed again." He moved from behind his desk, seeming to vacuum the last wisps of air from her lungs. "Now, if that is all, I have important things to attend to."

She stood rooted inside the doorway as he advanced on her. She felt as if she was staring at an incoming train.

He brushed against her as he left, leaving her buried under the debris of every belief she'd held dear. About him and her father. About herself.

It had all been a *deal*.

"I want to know everything, Mr. Saunders."

"I thought you were aware of the basics, Ms. Gra…" Ethan Saunders, her father's attorney, halted on the other end of the line. "Excuse me. Princess Aal Ferjani."

Princess Aal Ferjani. She'd never felt this name applied to her. She'd thought it was because of the state of her marriage. Now she knew it was because it didn't apply. And it never would.

"*Sabrina* will do, Mr. Saunders," she said tightly. "And I want to know more than the basics. I want every detail. There are no legal provisos that stop you from filling me in, are there?"

"When you put it that way, no," the man said cautiously. "I just got the impression that your father didn't want to bother you with particulars. I assumed that was why you weren't present during negotiations or contract signing."

Wading deeper into the nightmare, needing to hit rock bottom and be done with it, she prodded, "I do need to be bothered with the particulars, Mr. Saunders. My future depends on it."

There was a protracted silence on the other end. Then he exhaled. "Very well, Sabrina. While you were involved in your graduate studies, your father's health deteriorated, plunging him into a deep depression. He made catastrophic financial decisions—against my advisement, I must add. They ruined him. It was then that Sheikh Adham moved in. He'd been circling your father's land, and had tried to purchase it more than once. He knew he could finally acquire the land he'd long coveted with your father no longer in a position to refuse the sale. He had clear plans to close down the winery and plant other crops, while using the rest of the unplanted land as a horse farm.

"But your father was not without his own strategy. He investigated Sheikh Adham in turn, learning of his need to produce an heir within a certain time frame."

Her heart detonated at the confirmation of her worst fears. "And he offered me to him."

"You did fulfill all of Sheikh Adham's requirements,

and your father was still an astute enough businessman to know that. You are of impeccable lineage, physical qualities and…reputation."

Sabrina felt another red-hot lance skewering through her.

So that was why Adham had pretended to want her. He'd been out to assure her purity when he'd taken her for a test drive before deciding to marry her. A test drive he'd hoped would bear his required fruit, that he'd been loath to perform, judging by his aversion to repeating it, except when necessity dictated.

He'd been another of her father's arranged grooms all along.

But he'd gone far beyond any of them ever had. He'd seduced her to make sure she'd consent to the marriage. The mutually beneficial deal. For her father and for him.

And instead of being an heiress, she was actually indebted to him and would regain her legacy only when she provided him with a child. A child he wanted in order to fulfill his father's demands.

He'd never wanted to marry her, and felt nothing sincere for her. She was nothing to him.

No. She was worse than nothing. She was an annoyance, a burden. One he probably would get rid of the moment he could.

Mr. Saunders was going on about fine print. She'd heard all she'd wanted to hear, all she couldn't bear hearing. She didn't notice when the call ended. She might have hung up on the man.

It was worse than she'd feared. She'd been the only one under the misconception that this was a real marriage. Everyone else knew what it was—another of Adham's breeding ventures.

She'd been offered and accepted as a desirable mare.

But worse, Adham had believed all along that she was in on the deal.

Rage rose inside her again. She wiped fiercely at the tears.

It didn't matter what he'd believed. Only one thing mattered. He had to know she wanted no part of his plan, had agreed to none of it. She'd take nothing from him. She'd do anything, give up everything, to prove it.

And if fate should have it that she gave him his coveted heir, it would be on her terms, not his. She'd make sure her child didn't grow up a pawn in a royal chess game like her—or a heartless, cold-blooded manipulator like him.

Five

Adham swung the mallet with such force he catapulted the ball off the field, sending mud and grass exploding in the air.

How dare she.

Acting the neglected wife. Taking him to task about not fulfilling his marital duties. As if she'd ever wanted more from him than his wealth and status.

But he knew otherwise.

It had all been a tightly woven plot between her and her father. It was why he couldn't bring himself to touch her again, even though the lust he'd felt from the moment he'd laid eyes on her was intensifying, was corroding his restraint. And damn her, every time he saw her, the wholesomeness of her beauty, which needed no enhancements, overrode his senses. He didn't even have to see her. He only had to close his eyes to see her stunning honey-tan skin, to feel it beneath his hands, his lips, to imagine the waterfall of glossy mahogany hair sifting between his itching fingers, to remember her mesmerizing chocolate eyes gleaming with passion and her flushed lips trembling with pleasure. He woke up in a cold sweat every night, aching, remembering how her voluptuous body had exuded sensuality out of every pore, a sensuality he'd once thought unconscious. How she had wrapped around him, writhed beneath him. It was almost impossible not to storm her bedroom every night and lose himself inside her again.

Just before he'd met her, he'd been about to tell his father that he'd never take a wife by command like that. Then she'd walked into her father's hospital room and into his life, and suddenly the idea of marriage was no longer abhorrent to him, becoming all he could think of. The more he'd seen of her, the more he'd become convinced the fates had conspired to bring him his bride, the one woman he could contemplate having children with.

Then he'd taken her. And if he'd had any uncertainties or hesitations about her, her honest and limitless passion, the unprecedented intimacy he'd experienced with her, the unimaginable pleasure, what she'd so explicitly shown and told him had been reciprocated in full, had solidified his resolve, sealed his fate.

The next day, while Sabrina slept in his bed, he'd gone to Thomas Grant, to ask him for her hand in marriage. But the man had spoken first. And Adham had realized.

Grant had targeted him as the best groom for his daughter and the surest way out of his debts. And he'd set Sabrina on him. All her artlessness, her eagerness for his company, her hunger for him had been an undetectable act. And it had worked. Spectacularly.

But Grant had grown desperate in his illness. He'd thought he could no longer afford to let things develop at their own pace, to maintain the illusion of spontaneity. So he'd exposed their plan, laying it out in distasteful terms of give and take.

The wretched man must have been in worse shape than anyone had realized, or else he'd seriously underestimated his daughter's seductive powers. He'd asked for far less than what Adham had been resolved to offer when he'd thought he was pursuing a marriage built on mutual desire.

Adham had been so enraged, his first reaction was to snatch everything from father and daughter, leaving them with neither land nor deal. But pity for Grant's desperation had won. Not to mention lust for Sabrina. Even though he'd hated himself for it, he could think of nothing but repeating that night of delirium—and that even more addicting morning after.

Then Grant had died, and Sabrina had been broken up over his death. And although he'd discovered her deception and manipulation, he had recognized her anguish as real. He couldn't have assuaged his lust for her, no matter how it had gnawed at him. Not even when she'd let him know he could. Especially when she had. He'd been disgusted—with her, with himself—and conflicted about her bereavement, enraged at his decisions, his desires. He'd thought it safest to stay away from her until he regained his sanity and decided how to deal with it all.

But the more he let time pass, the more he realized it had been a grave mistake to marry her. He desired her for real, while she desired him only as a sponsor to maintain her family name and boost her lifestyle. He'd never paid for his pleasures and he'd be damned if he'd start with her. Not even if she was the one woman he craved. Especially since she was.

But he couldn't even let her go, washing his hands of this sordid mess. He'd trapped himself forever.

Men in his family married for life, if at all possible.

Even if separation occurred, it remained private, with a solid family front presented, for the sake of all but the couple. Considerations far bigger ruled. The royal family's traditions, Khumayrah's veneration of marriage, the Aal Ferjanis' allies and rivals. A man who wasn't bound to the wife he'd chosen and the family he'd made with her couldn't be trusted.

Which brought him to that heir his father had revealed was necessary to help stabilize the currently volatile internal affairs in their kingdom.

For that alone, he couldn't let anyone suspect that his marriage was a mere business deal. It would be the perfect way for his enemies to slander him.

They had done it to his father, spreading rumors that Adham and his younger sister weren't his, that his bargained wife had cheated. The repercussions had been far-reaching, and it had taken half of Adham's life to disprove the lies and wipe clean their stain.

This alone should have stopped him from following in his father's footsteps. His parents' marriage had developed into a love match, but this wasn't his own situation, and he should have factored in that if the conditions of his marriage were exposed, it would affect the royal house and the kingdom's stability.

So here he was. Trapped into playing the doting, replete groom. And to his fury, his desire for her, having his eyes and hands all over her in public, hadn't been an act. The act had been the distance he'd forced on them in private, the disinterest and detachment he'd pretended when she'd confronted him.

B'Ellahi, that confrontation. He'd used up his last drop of will holding himself back from pouncing on her, dragging her to the ground and giving her what she'd been indignantly pretending to demand. His mind roiled still with conjectures over why she had.

He again slammed into the same conclusion. That she'd become worried. She hadn't seen the contracts, and had probably been trying to find out if their terms were worth the act she'd been putting on. After all, she'd made a tremendous effort so far, and hadn't missed a beat since they'd met.

But now that he'd assured her of the extent of her gains from their arrangement, she'd resume playing her part with even more commitment. This past week, her performance had surpassed his wildest expectations. He'd felt her dissolving in his arms, inundating him with hunger, with urgent need for everything he'd do to her....

How is she faking all this?

A thought struck him with the force of a mallet to the head.

What if she wasn't? What if, apart from her mercenary motives for their marriage, she lusted after him for real?

If this was true, it changed everything....

"Adham. Earth to Adham."

He raised burning eyes to the booming voice. He found he'd come to a full stop in the middle of the field with Nicolas staring at him in surprise and concern. He and the other players were wiping off the clumps of mud and grass they were covered in.

"The game is right here, buddy." Jacob Anders, who played his team's number one position, smirked. "But it's clear you're not."

"*Sí,*" Nicolas agreed. "Why don't we resume our practice when you don't feel the urge to take whatever's eating you on the lawn and pelt us with it?"

Adham grimaced at his teammates. He wasn't up to their teasing. He swung Layl away and galloped off the field.

They were right. He had to take this out on the cause of his turmoil. On Sabrina.

If she wanted him, she was going to get him.

If mind-blowing pleasure was all they could have out of this "deal," then they'd have it. They'd never stop having it.

He snapped his cell phone out, pressing her speed-dial number.

Her phone rang until the line disconnected. He dialed again immediately. Four more disconnections later, and he was ready to commit violence.

She answered the fifth time. Or rather, the line opened. She said nothing.

But he could feel her on the other end. He could swear he felt her breath flaying his face in its heat and sweetness.

He growled with a spike of anger and arousal, "Why didn't you answer right away?"

Silence on her end. Then her unsteady inhalation skewered his brain, forked more steel into his erection. How he remembered those fractured breaths that had driven him mad as he'd plunged inside her....

"I answered now." Her voice was clipped, distant, yet it was still the mellow caress he'd replayed in his memory nonstop, crooning her need for him, crying out as her urgency rose, sharpening with the pain of his first invasion, then losing all inhibition as he occupied her, as her pleasure peaked. "Anything you want?"

I want everything, he wanted to roar.

But he *was* going to get everything. Starting tonight. No more holding back. For any reason. For better and probably for worse than he could imagine, she was his wife. And he planned to gorge himself on all the advantages of that fact. He'd suffer the disadvantages gladly when he had her total abandon to negate it all.

Her father's bargain might have blinded him for a while, but he could see clearly now. There was no way she'd faked her responses. Her soul might be that of a mercenary, but her body was that of a hedonist. But what mattered was that he was convinced now that she suffered his same predicament. She craved the pleasure only he could bring her.

"Sebastian is holding a gala party tonight in the VIP tent," he said, his voice thick with pent-up hunger. "It's to celebrate our marriage. It's imperative we show our hosts that we appreciate their thoughtfulness and efforts."

After another protracted silence, she asked expressionlessly, "How do you suggest we do that?"

"Sebastian requested that we attend the party in full royal garb. Have Hasnaa advise you on how to dress. I'll send you outfits and sets of jewelry to choose from. I want you to be my princess tonight."

Another silence stretched in the wake of his directives. Then a tremulous inhalation spilled from lips he knew to be petal soft and cherry flushed and dewy. He hardened beyond agony. "Anything else?"

"Yes," she hissed with the abrasion of arousal, the knowledge that it would be unendurable hours before he could assuage it. "Don't straighten or restrain your hair. Leave its curls wild."

She muttered what he assumed was an agreement, then hung up.

He stared at the phone as if he expected her to call back, to say more. He knew she wouldn't.

The dynamics between them had changed. Just hours ago there'd been no acknowledgement of how it was between them. Now it was out in the open, and she'd dropped the adoring-bride act in private.

But her indignation this morning had been about

more than her worry for her future—it had contained true frustration. No matter why they'd ended up married, she'd expected him, *wanted* him, to wallow in the carnal connection they shared.

That must be the reason behind her standoffishness just now. She must think he still intended to deprive her of what she needed.

She'd be relieved that he'd decided to disregard how she and her father had set him up and would drag her into the tumults of passion. At every opportunity.

And if they'd attained that much pleasure when he'd been so careful with her, when she'd been so untried, now that he could unleash his passion…well, he couldn't even imagine how it would be between them. In fact, exacting retribution on her through sensual torment would only take it all to explosive levels.

Starting tonight.

"I think you've chosen the outfit that best showcases your beauty, *ya Ameerah* Sabrina."

Sabrina caught the genial Khumayran woman's eyes in the mirror. Hasnaa was truly a beauty, as her name proclaimed her to be. She was Jameel's wife and now her head lady-in-waiting.

She attempted a smile, to thank her for her reassurance. She could see for herself it came out a grimace.

Thankfully, Hasnaa didn't notice her forced attempt as she fussed around her, adjusting her outfit. It was the first time that Sabrina had availed herself of Hasnaa's services. And only because Adham had demanded it.

He wanted her to be his princess tonight. To look the part, that was. She felt obligated to meet his demand. To honor the pact that her father had made. She wouldn't give Adham a chance to say a Grant didn't uphold her end of a deal. Even if she herself felt there was nothing more to uphold, felt mired in a nightmare she'd never wake up from. A prison her father and Adham had conspired to throw her into.

She'd felt desperation before, with each loss in her life. But each time, she'd forged on, because there had always been something to strive for, someone else who mattered. Someone who'd been there for her, too.

When her mother died when she was twelve, she turned her grief into more love for her father, even though it wasn't easy being his daughter, especially after his bereavement made him even more ultra-protective of her. Then years passed and she realized the hardest part of being his daughter had nothing to do with his actions and everything to do with who he was.

She realized the magnitude of the problem when she entered college. She lost count of the men who pursued her for her father's assets. To make things worse, her father, in his attempts to protect her from opportunists, started supplying one suitable bachelor after another. She considered those men not much better than the vultures, since they also wanted to acquire her because of her father's assets, if in a merger rather than a takeover.

So she told him that she wasn't interested in marriage, but in graduate studies and a career.

After years of pursuing her with insistence that marriage didn't preclude a career, Thomas gave up, leaving her to her plans. She now realized he only did because he'd plunged into depression and debt. Then, just after she obtained her degrees, he had his heart attack.

But all through her dread and desperation, she'd been strong for him. Then he'd died. But Adham had been there, and she wasn't alone. She had him. Or so she'd thought.

She *was* alone. She had no one. Certainly not Adham.

She gazed at her reflection in the gold-framed, full-length mirror. It felt like she was looking at herself inside a gilded cage. Completing the picture of captive luxury was one of the outfits he'd sent her. They'd all been beyond breathtaking. Not that she'd appreciated their exquisiteness. She hadn't chosen the outfit she was wearing now, discerning that it would best suit her as Hasnaa had implied. She'd dragged it haphazardly off the rack.

She looked at it now, seeing it for the first time. A ravishing red outfit that blended all the ornate lushness of Adham's native Khumayran culture with stunning modern twists.

The sarilike, handmade, intricately worked and embroidered creation and its *dupatta*—what Hasnaa was now busily securing over her "wild curls"—were a masterpiece. A dream of silk, georgette and organza worked in fine gold threads, semiprecious stones, sequins, cutwork, mirror, pearl and crystal work.

To top it all off was one of the sets of jewelry he'd sent her. Hasnaa had chosen for her what she deemed went best with her outfit, a set consisting of two necklaces—a choker and a longer piece that framed her cleavage to maximum effect—earrings that reached to her shoulders, and bangles that covered half of her right forearm. Each piece had carefully cut and polished multicolored gemstones embedded into delicate twenty-four karat gold.

And to think she'd thought he was being indulgent when she'd found the enormous collection lining that extensive dressing room. She'd felt uncomfortable, accepting all that, even from the husband who could afford endless luxuries. She hadn't wanted the shadow of materialistic considerations between them. But she'd reluctantly conceded it was part of looking the part in appearances vital to his status.

But now she knew the truth. This wasn't an indulgence.

This was part of her price.

And she was to wear it, like a tag. Another check on his status report.

A bubble of nausea pushed against her diaphragm. She thanked and dismissed Hasnaa, and collapsed on the nearest chair the moment the door closed. She lowered her forehead to her knees.

She fought back a wave of sickness that seemed to rise from her soul. Suspicion struck her, deepening her distress.

This could be what Adham had hoped for.

She could be pregnant. It would be so easy to find out.

She couldn't find out. Not yet. She didn't want to know one way or another when she asked him to end their pact.

But first, she had to play the delirious bride again.

This time she would indeed have to act.

But it would be the last time she did.

Six

"Oh, my, Sabrina. You look a-*mazing!*" Julia exclaimed, her chocolate-brown eyes wide with admiration.

"You look like a princess right out of a fairy tale!" Catherine exclaimed, awe sparkling in her eyes.

"Okay, the verdict is in!" Vanessa Hughes, Sebastian's sister, said as she finished her inspection of Sabrina, looking every bit the fashionista with her killer body wrapped in a gold second-skin, plunging-neck, floor-length gown. "This is the most incredible outfit I've ever seen in my life!"

Sabrina flashed a smile at the women she'd come to like immensely, a smile as genuine as her condition allowed. "You are just too kind, ladies. I feel like a prize idiot here, coming all dressed up as if for a masquerade, while you're all floating around looking like supermodels fresh off the runway."

"Are you kidding?" Vanessa scoffed. "I'd give anything for an outfit like that. But I doubt I'd carry it off half as well as you do. You have that exotic tinge to your looks, that…heat to your coloring—you just set the whole thing on fire."

"See?" Sabrina smiled again. "Too kind, I tell you. But let me say something else. All the ego boosting is very much appreciated."

"As if you need our ego boosting," Julia said, winking, "with a man like Sheikh Adham, who has the female population drooling, literally composing odes in homage to your charms."

"*And* accompanying every word of his sonnets with a white-hot look," Vanessa added. "The guy showers you with more ego boosts than most women could handle."

"Ah, those hot-blooded desert princes." Julia sighed. "If only our men were that demonstrative and vocal."

"But Sheikh Adham is far from being either," Catherine, who knew Adham well, interjected. "He's certainly the best employer I could ask for, but in my opinion, reserved and uncommunicative are his middle and last names."

"Then this is an even greater testament to your charms, Sabrina." Vanessa held her hands together beneath her chin in a swooning gesture. "And their effect on him. I've never seen a man so overtly in love before!"

Each word hit Sabrina like a whip. She wanted to beg them to stop, to tell them that he'd only been putting on a show. That it had fooled them, these intelligent, discerning women. Just as it had fooled her. Until he'd slammed her with the truth about his emotions—or rather, his lack of them.

The memory of his passionless gaze as he'd decimated her world lanced through her once more. She felt her smile splintering, its cracked edges driving into her flesh.

She had to excuse herself before the heat pricking behind her eyes dissolved into an unstoppable flood.

Yeah, that would ruin her image as "his princess."

Perhaps she shouldn't fight the tears after all.

No. She wasn't only his so-called princess, she was a Grant. Foremost, she was herself. She didn't break down. Not in public. And she *would* stop doing it in private. She was done letting him control her emotions, her life. She was taking control, as of now.

"And I thought *you* looked right out of *Arabian Nights,* Adham."

Sabrina swung around at hearing Sebastian's amused comment. He faded from her awareness the moment she registered him.

Adham was beside him. Adham as she'd never seen him. In the garb that revealed what he was underneath the projection of modernity, the polish of advancement.

A raider of the desert who seized whatever he wanted, made willing slaves of his conquests, whose ruthlessness was only matched by the heartlessness of his seduction. A being from another world where everything was laced with mystery and magic, edged by danger, drenched in excess, in passion.

In a pitch-black *abaya* that spread over his endless shoulders and billowed around him like a shroud of mystery, a high-collared top embroidered with *zari* gold thread, and pants fitted into leather boots, he looked like a supernatural being who descended to earth to rule, to conquer, an avenging angel from the realm of oriental fables.

She swallowed. What felt like ground glass slid down her throat. His beauty, his majesty…hurt. Her stupidity, in believing he'd fallen for her as totally as she had for him, hurt more.

"I did tell you to wait until you saw Sabrina, Seb," Adham murmured as his arm snaked around her waist, his hand dipping beneath her top's edge to singe her flesh with the heat of his electricity-wielding fingers. "But even I couldn't have imagined how spellbinding the trappings of my culture could be until her beauty and grace adorned them."

Her instinctive reaction was to swoon at the extravagance of his praise, to melt into the possession of his touch. It took all of three heartbeats before reality sank its fangs into her and had her lurching away as if from burning tentacles.

Adham's eyes didn't betray any change of expression, apart from the fluctuation in his pupils' size. Without missing a beat, he pulled her to him again, as if he hadn't realized she'd pulled away. Or maybe he wouldn't let her in front of those whose opinion mattered to him. "I hope I didn't leave you waiting long, *ya jameelati*. I should have escorted you here or at least been here to receive you, to be the first to look on your enchantment tonight. But there was an emergency with one of the ponies."

"What?" Catherine eyes widened, her smile fractured, alarm catching her off guard. "What happened? Which pony?"

"Rahawan," Adham answered, sparing her a glance before returning his sizzling focus to Sabrina. "He had severe colic. I called Dr. Lima and stayed until Rahawan started recovering."

"Oh, I'll go."

This made Adham relinquish his hold over Sabrina's eyes, stretch an arm in Catherine's way, cutting her movement short. "Of course you won't, Catherine."

"But I am still working for you until the end of the season," Catherine protested. "Even if I weren't, your horses will always be mine, too, Sheikh Adham. I have to make sure he's all right."

"He is. But thanks for your continued caring and

commitment. Richard is a lucky man to have such a loyal, compassionate woman. Now put your mind at ease and enjoy the party. I intend to." He turned to Sabrina, hugging her closer. "Now that I'm with you, it's a certainty that I will." He looked to the women. "May I borrow my bride, ladies? It's been a long day without her."

The women giggled and fanned themselves, winking at her as he swept her away.

Once they were out of earshot, she tried to step back from his embrace, struggling to make it look like she wasn't pushing him away. He only tightened his hold, bearing down on her with his heat and voracity. His fake voracity.

He bent to take her lips. She turned her head at the last second. His lips latched on her cheek instead. He burned it with his kiss. "I thought I could wait for later, but I can't."

She pushed harder at him, managing to put him at arm's length. "Listen, nobody can hear you now, so you can quit it."

"Quit what?"

"The act. Go light on the theatrics. Less is more and all that. Look around and learn from your friends how a man in love is supposed to behave. Sebastian and Richard are not oozing all over their women."

"Oozing?" His frown was spectacular.

"Yes, oozing. You better watch it. You're crossing from convincing underacting to ridiculous overacting."

His glower deepened. Then something flared over his features, so sexual and savage she felt her core melt in ferocious response.

"Suheeh?" he drawled, slow and devastating, a predator certain his mate was in the bag, certain he could prolong her torment and his gratification to his heart's content.

"Really? The only under and over I'm interested in are when they involve you and me during lovemaking. So let's drop all acting and get down to the truth." He tugged her hand and brought her slamming against his steel length. One hand splayed across her back, searing the flesh exposed by the dipping back of her top through the sheer *dupatta* covering it, the other hand sinking into her left buttock, yanking her to him, grinding her against his thigh. A moan of unwilling stimulation bubbled from her depths. Her head fell back, her mouth opened, her lips stung and swelled as if he'd already ravished them. He documented her reaction, merciless satisfaction blazing in his eyes. "*This* is the only truth. That you want me. As much as I want you."

She tried to break free, feeling as if she were drowning. As she was—in sensation, in yearning. Every syllable he uttered, every press of his fingers, every abrasion of his clothes on her exposed skin, every gust of his breath brushing any oversensitive part of her, was an aphrodisiac overdose. She felt she was being submerged in him, in her need for him.

It made her angrier.

He was only manipulating her, feeling nothing himself. And she'd be damned if she'd let him pull her strings like that.

She wrenched free, any attempt to make this look like anything but an all-out fight dissipating.

For she was fighting. For her sanity, her sense of self. What he was taking over, with such ease, just because he could, not because he wanted her.

"Oh, no, you don't," she spat. "You told me how it is this morning. You don't get to change the rules as you please. I don't know why you're doing this and I don't care. Just let go of me."

He hauled her back, crashed her into him once again, his arms a vise. "I'm never letting go of you."

She stilled in his arms, chagrin and embarrassment drenching her. "For God's sake, stop. Everyone's watching us."

"Let them watch."

"But this isn't what you want them to watch. At least, if you don't let me go, it won't be."

"Is this how you want to play it now, Sabrina? You want me to make you succumb, take it out of your hands? You want me to arouse you out of your mind and take you so you can have what you want and not be responsible? I'd be happy to oblige. I made you beg for me once. This time, I won't have to take it easy or go slow, to make allowances for your inexperience and discomfort. This time I can show you just how much you inflame me and hold nothing back, exploiting every inch of your made-for-pleasure body, giving you so much satisfaction you'll faint with it."

She felt the world distorting, as if she'd pass out from testosterone overexposure. She struggled to focus, choking, "Stop it, Adham. If you don't, I *will* make a scene. And not the kind of scene you want your friends and the paparazzi to witness."

The sensuality on his face deepened as he leaned back, his hands shaping her, exploring her curves, cascading fire through every cell. He stopped at her breasts, kneaded and weighed them, rubbed circles of insanity around her nipples through the layered material of her top. "Show me, Sabrina. Do your worst."

A second before she felt she'd faint for real, she smacked his hands off her and spun around.

She didn't get far. He caught her at the tent's entrance, turned her and snatched her off her feet. His hands clamped her back, her buttocks, opening her thighs in her flaring *lehenga* over his hips. One hand held her in place as the other snatched her *dupatta* out of the way to sink into her curls, holding her face upturned to his, her neck arched back.

He swooped down to latch his lips on her pulse, growling against its frantic beating, his voice feral. "I shouldn't want you, I should keep this cold and all business. But you inflamed me, drove me mad, from that first moment I laid eyes on you. *W'hada gabl mat'sallemeeli nafssek—* And this was before you surrendered yourself to me. *Men hada'l yaum w'ana fen'nar—*I've been in hell since that day, craving you and knowing I shouldn't. But I don't care anymore why we married. You're caught in the same trap, you crave me just as much. And desire this fierce can't be denied."

Everything stilled inside her, desperation and anguish extinguished like a candle in a hurricane.

He wanted her, too? It hadn't been an act to make her succumb to his plans? He'd tried to keep it business, but his desire for her was overriding his intentions and his control?

If this was true, then his desire was fiercer than anything she'd wished for. This meant there was hope for their marriage. Far more hope than she'd dared imagine.

"Adham…I don't…"

He misinterpreted what she'd started saying and overrode her. "You do. I can feel your desire, can sense it. Your body is humming with need for me against your will—seeking, offering, begging for mine. I can feel your heart racing mine, your blood thundering below my fingertips."

She would have been mortified that he could read her reactions so explicitly if her reserves of mortification hadn't been depleted thinking of the scandal they were creating.

And if she didn't want him to know how he made her feel. But now she did.

Then everything ceased. Adham wrenched his lips from her neck, raising his head only to swoop down again to claim her mouth.

She cried out at the feel of his heat and moistness, of his tongue driving inside her, rubbing against hers. His growls poured into her, welling in surges of pleasure throughout her body.

He finished her, drained her, layering arousal in bolts to her breasts, her gut, her core. Heat built until she writhed with it, opening herself up, inviting his domination.

He raised her, brought his erection grinding into her long-molten core. Sensation sharpened, cleaving a cry from her depths.

And despite the pounding in her head, the shearing from her lungs and his, she felt it.

The commotion of curiosity and amusement and disbelief. The shuffling and whirs and flashes of people rushing to document their mindless disregard of everything but their conflagration.

He raised his head, his eyes almost black and unseeing as they panned the crowd surrounding them. Then, with a growl, he bent, hauling her high in his arms.

"I'm taking you home, Sabrina." His words held the conviction and power of a pledge. "And I'm making you mine, in every way. Tonight and forever."

Seven

Sabrina clung to Adham's neck as he strode out of the tent, the whole world receding from her awareness, shrinking to the confines of his body.

She registered nothing but its powerful perfection moving against hers with his every stride, his hands rhythmically squeezing her flesh. She saw his face clenched on such drive and felt weakness invading her every muscle, in preparation to have all this ferocity unleashed on her.

She didn't know how long he'd walked or what distance he'd covered. Time was suspended, space was compacted, until she found herself inside a limo with dark windows and a soundproof, mirrored partition. Adham laid her down and came to rest on top of her. Her legs opened in eagerness to accommodate his bulk. He lay over her, giving her what she needed of his weight, supporting enough of it so as not to oppress her. He devoured her lips, his hands everywhere, creating erogenous zones all over her, his hips driving between her splayed thighs in a simulation of the possession she was quaking for.

She heard her voice, thick and choppy, pleading for him. He rose off her, dragging her up. She swayed with the car's smooth movement as it shot across the streets, with the imbalance he'd struck inside her, feeling as if the burn in her blood would consume her if she didn't get under his skin.

"Sabrina, *galbi,* I need to feel your desire, taste your pleasure."

Before she could understand what he meant or tell him he could do whatever he liked with her, he hauled her on his lap, her back to his front, her thighs splitting wide over one of his. He stretched back so her upper body fell to the side and into the curve of his left arm. His hands came around her, undoing her front fastening.

She moaned his name as her breasts spilled out of the imprisonment of the corsetlike top and into his hands. He bent, leaning around her, engulfing one nipple and then the other in the moist heat of his mouth. Her cries rose, lengthened, her writhing getting more frantic. He didn't give her a chance to process the feelings as his right hand dragged her *lehenga* up, yanking her panties down. Then his palm was cupping her mound, squeezing it, condensing the throbbing there into a pinpoint of insanity.

He let go before it all spilled over. In her haze, she realized. He knew that she needed intimacy, not release. And he was giving it to her. The closeness of owning her flesh as intimately as she did.

Two strong, certain fingers parted her feminine lips, delving into the desire flowing there for him. He lifted his head from her breasts to swallow her sobs of overstimulation. He glided in her moistness, from her bud to her opening, until she bucked, begged. Only then he slid inside her, adding a third finger, replacing his fingers at her bud with his thumb. Her keen poured into his mouth. He withdrew his fingers, corkscrewing the tension inside her to a weeping pitch.

"Take your pleasure, *ya jameelati. Areeni jamalek wenti b'tjeeli*…show me your beauty as you come for me."

She'd been trying to hold back, needing to come with him deep inside her. But he was, if in another way. And he wanted her to give him this surrender. She'd give him anything he wanted.

He thrust his fingers back in, along with his tongue deep inside her mouth. And the tension snapped, over and over, uncoiling then folding back on itself, only to lash out again as her orgasm quaked through her like the ebb and flow of a stormy sea.

His gaze bathed her in his possessiveness, in his profoundly male satisfaction at the sight of her racked with pleasure, begging to be at his total mercy, to be taken, pleasured any way he could think of.

He held his fingers deep inside her, letting her quiver to the last tremor of satisfaction around them, before he slowly removed them, brought them up to his lips, licked them, growling his enjoyment at tasting her.

He gathered her, folded her, held her tight in his arms. His eyes were incandescent in the dimness, flaring gold with each passing streetlight filtering through the darkened windows.

"Do you know what it is, seeing and feeling you taking your fill of the pleasure I bring you, *ya hayati?* Tasting it? It's the most beautiful thing in my world."

Her heart swelled so hard, so fast, she whimpered with it. She couldn't utter a word. She'd been at her lowest point, and had given up on him. She'd been trying to contemplate a life of emotional exile, loving him and knowing he'd never love her back.

Now he'd given her this. And it wasn't only sex, or pleasure. He was opening himself up to her, letting her see inside him. This was for her, not for the eyes and ears of the world. And it was sincere. She just knew it was.

Tenderness swamped her, welled from her in feverish kisses and caresses all over his face. He rumbled a string of native praises to her as he kissed and caressed her in return.

The car stopped. In seconds he'd helped fasten her top and had her out and in his arms.

He took her where she'd thought she'd never be—the room he'd chosen as his in this sprawling house.

It was not as enormous or extravagantly decorated as the one he'd given her, but because it was permeated by his scent and presence, it was in a class of its own. Any place where he chose to live his most private moments was the best place she'd ever been.

He laid her down at the foot of his bed and proceeded to strip from her the outfit and jewelry in excruciating slowness, pausing at every inch of flesh he exposed to fondle and worship and praise. By the time he had her naked, her teeth were clattering, her heart in hyperdrive, desperate for an end to the sensual torment.

He then stood up to admire her sight, arranged among black silk pillows and sheets. Then, as if he hadn't tormented her enough, he started his own striptease.

He first shrugged off the silk *abaya*. It slid from his daunting shoulders and slithered to the floor with a resigned sigh. His gold-embroidered top, wrapped cummerbund and boots followed. He left the low-riding loose pants on.

Before she could cry out her indignation, he kneeled before her. His hands traveled up legs that went boneless at his first touch, his to do with as he chose. It pleased him to spread them, to drag her by them, to bring them over his shoulders.

"*Daheenah adoogek men jedd*—now I taste you for real. I've been addicted to your taste from that first time. I've been starving for more of you." He opened her lips, gave her core one long lick, groaning in response to her cry. "Say you'll always let me taste you, always want me to."

She wanted to tell him but her tongue twisted in her mouth, paralyzed with anticipation. She only keened, her hair falling all over her face with the vigorousness of her nod. Satisfied with her condition, with her response, he clamped her feminine lips in a devouring kiss. He licked and suckled at her swollen flesh, thrust inside her with his tongue, drank deep of her pleasure. He took her to the edge again and again, only to pull her back, set her to a simmer, then build her desperation once more until she felt the ache inside her reaching critical mass. She begged him with her hands in his hair, with her body writhing in mounting agony as she tried to pull him up, to have him penetrate her, ride her, put her out of her misery.

He resisted her, lashed her trigger and sent her convulsing and shrieking into another racking orgasm.

He drank her dry, kept licking her, soothing, defusing the surplus of sensations, until her oversensitized flesh subsided. And she wanted him more than ever.

She struggled to her elbows, looked down on the magnificent sight he made, kneeling between her legs, his lion's head rubbing her thighs, his lips worshipping them. Her heart spilled a fresh batch of palpitations.

"Adham, stop tormenting me. Don't make me wait anymore."

He raised eyes blazing with satisfaction at her renewed agitation, at his own pent-up arousal. He rose, pushing her back across the bed with his shoulders against her legs until he had her in the middle. Then he rose above her on all fours.

"Release me."

At his command, though her hands felt like they were no longer under her control, she fumbled with his pants. She somehow undid the zipper and pushed them halfway down his muscled thighs, exposing their bronzed splendor. He took pity on her, pushed them all the way down, kicked them off. He held her hands and guided them into removing his tight boxers. And she gasped.

His erection sprang hard and long and heavy, slamming against his belly. Just the sight exacerbated her swooning state.

He noted her reaction with those all-seeing eyes as he again had his hands and lips all over her triggers.

"I pleasured you in the car, and again now," he groaned against her nipples, her pulses, her lips, "not only because I crave your pleasure as much and more than I do mine, but because I need to know that your desire is all mine, all about needing *my* possession. Tell me."

"I want you," she moaned. "I've been going out of my mind with wanting you. I want you all the time, doing everything to me. Please, Adham, *habibi*, take me."

He rose to loom over her, a god of virility and beauty, almost menacing in the fierceness of his focus, the ferocity of his lust. He pushed her with gentle power until she lay flat beneath the cage of his muscle and maleness. He drove one knee between hers, winding the throbbing between her thighs to a tighter rhythm.

"How do you want me to take you? The first time?"

She didn't hesitate. She knew just how. "Fill my arms, let me wrap myself around you as you fill me."

"And the second?"

"Cover me, lie on top of me, over my back, let me feel all of you pressing me into the bed as you possess me."

He bent to pull hard on one nipple, grazing the other with his blunt fingernail. "And the third and fourth and fifth time?"

Her delirium intensified with each suckle and flick. "Anything—anything at all. Just do it all."

He rose over her again. "Then give it to me. Everything you have, everything you are. I will have it all."

"Yes. *Yes.*" She stabbed her fingers into the mane raining around his face, brought him down to her for a compulsive kiss. She tore her lips away, needing to know, panting. "And you'll give it all to me, too?"

"All that I have. All that I am. It's all yours, *ya malekati,* my owner. Take it. Take me. All of me." He reared back between her splayed thighs, his erection throbbing over her mound and reaching up to her belly button, heavy and engorged. He glided its underside between her lips, nudging her trigger over and over. She arched up, opening herself, hurrying him. He only rose on one knee, taking her one desire out of reach. "Show me what you want."

Unable to heed any inhibition, unable to wait to take advantage of the freedom he was offering her, she reached a trembling hand to his erection. She couldn't close around his girth. Intimidation shuddered through her even as another surge of readiness flooded her core. She stroked the velvet-over-steel shaft in wonder, rubbing the smooth head with the fluid silk seeping from its slit, her tongue tingling with the need to taste it. Promising herself she'd beg for the privilege later, she tugged at his shaft.

He growled, deep and dark, thrust his hips at her, watching her with an intensity she felt left its marks all over her skin. He let her drag him closer to her sex, still keeping his eyes on hers. But with the first touch of their intimate flesh, he threw his head back in an agonized growl, a duet with her keen. Then, as if they'd agreed, they both lowered their gazes to the sight of the intimacy she was performing.

She slid his head along her inner lips, bathing it in her moistness. Unbearably aroused, rumbles reverberated from deep within him on every glide, a sharper cry from her each time it nudged her slit. She kept going on and on, until he was shaking as hard as she was, his breathing as labored as hers. She knew she'd tumble into oblivion any second now, had to do it with him buried deep inside her.

She could no longer hold herself up, could no longer bring her hand to close around him. She slumped back to the bed, legs splaying. His erection was throbbing at her opening where she'd left it before she lost all coordination.

"Please," she sobbed.

"Please what?" It came out the growl of a great feline at the end of his tether. "Tell me. Let me hear you say the words."

"Fill me."

Rumbling something driven, he did, on one lunge.

She wailed as her flesh yielded to his invasion, as he stretched her beyond capacity. He forged on through her molten core until she felt him reach her womb.

The coil of sensations that had compacted inside her unraveled so violently, it lashed out through her system, shredding her with a release so profound, she convulsed as if with a seizure, as if with a chain reaction of explosions. Gusts of sharpness shrieked from her depths on each detonation.

"*Sabrina.*" She felt him expand to a size she couldn't accommodate as he drove deeper inside her body, lodged into her recesses. She jerked like a marionette with her strings being pulled haphazardly, her inner walls squeezing him until he hissed. "*Aih, ya habibati, eeji alai*…come all over me."

And all that was left inside her was one need. She sobbed it. "Come with me…come inside me…fill me.…"

As if he'd been waiting for her plea, her command, his seed splashed against her spasming walls. She shook and wept as another breaker of pleasure crashed down on her with each jet hitting her most intimate flesh, as his erection shuddered inside her, as his roars of release harmonized with her cries.

Time expanded. The perfection of it. The totality. The oneness.

Pleasure raged, each slam of his inside her unhinging the foundations of her very soul until she felt he'd uprooted it, until she felt it roamed free, releasing her body of its limitations.

Then she slammed back to the bed beneath him. Aftershocks surged in a current inside her. He'd drained her of every spark her nervous system was capable of. She felt irrevocably sated.

But she knew better. He'd whisper in her ear, touch her with his gaze, beckon with his fingers and she'd go up in flames again.

He came down on top of her, letting her feel his beloved weight for a minute, before he twisted to his back, taking her with him, draping her over him like a blanket.

He caressed her back and hair, still hard inside her. "It was merciful I lived these past weeks with only the memory of our first night together. If I'd known that our belated wedding night would be a thousand times better, I would have probably lost my mind."

She smiled into his chest, gratification sweeping through her that his feelings so exactly echoed hers. "Or you might not have tormented us so long. If I'd known, I might have provoked you into losing your control much sooner."

"So you're admitting you provoked me on purpose."

She giggled. "If only I could claim that I did."

His chuckles revved below her ears as his arms tightened around her. Feeling him stir inside her, feeling her own body blossom once more for him, she sighed in contentment, "You know, you're overwhelming anyway, but in passion, you're annihilating."

"Look who's talking." In one swift move, he rolled her over, bringing her facedown as he mounted her from behind.

She arched into him, ready again, impatient. "That's not a complaint. I can't wait to be devastated, over and over."

And throughout the night and early morning hours, she was.

Eight

Sabrina opened her eyes in her husband's bed.

Adham. Her husband. For real. At last.

For several golden moments, tranquil and content, she lay there, savoring the knowledge, the soreness of satiation.

But it had been so much more than sex they'd shared. Adham had deep feelings for her. They might not be as complete as hers were for him, but they were pure and powerful. And they were growing. She'd make sure they never stopped.

They might have started out the wrong way, for the wrong reasons, but it didn't matter. They were right for each other. Perfect. And her love for him had broken through his preconceptions, had made him release all the emotion he'd struggled to suppress, thinking he shouldn't feel anything for her, his convenient bride.

She now relived the moments when she'd opened her

eyes hours ago, arched into his embrace, offered herself to him. Even three-quarters asleep, she'd been disappointed to feel clothes instead of his nakedness pressing down on her. He'd said he needed to see Sebastian, telling her to sleep off the exhaustion he'd caused her. She *had* blinked out the moment he'd closed the door.

But her battery was charged now. Overcharged. And there was no way she could bear waiting for him to come home.

She'd go bring him back to bed herself.

Thirty minutes later, she parked her car in the driveway of the Tudor-style Hughes Mansion.

She was let into a cathedral-ceiling hallway, and the butler informed her that Adham and Sebastian were in the living room. She told him to point her their way—she'd announce herself. She wanted to see Adham's reaction to her presence—the first surge of pleasure that would light his eyes—firsthand.

She approached the door, debating whether to knock or just enter. The decision was made for her when she found the door ajar. She was about to make her presence known when something Sebastian was saying froze her in her tracks.

"I have to give it to you, Adham, that was one hell of a show you put on yesterday. I can't buy publicity like that. The Bridgehampton Polo Club will not only be associated with priceless horses and A-list celebrities but with the drama of the uncontrollable passions of desert princes and their gorgeous, rebellious American wives. I project attendance will triple next year."

"Not that I'm unhappy the club might benefit from my actions," Adham said, "but that wasn't among the things on my mind yesterday."

"*If* you had anything on it at all, that is," Sebastian

teased, "apart from chasing down and capturing your defiant bride. Defiant at first, anyway. Then you caught her, kissed her and...whoosh. She went up in flames in your arms. I bet all those enemies who're watching you for proof that your marriage isn't real no longer have a leg to stand on."

There was a long moment of silence.

"How do you know about that?" Adham asked slowly.

"A sleazebag posing as a reporter came a few days ago to interview me, but mainly asked about you and your recent marriage. He tried to get me to give him anything that would paint your marriage as a business deal. He went on to say it's a common belief in your land that a bargained wife is an unsatisfied one who cheats to get back at the man who acquired her."

"It's not a belief, just a rationalization to explain cheating wives and an effective weapon to smear men in high places, since the greatest dishonor in my culture is to have a cheating wife. It is a death sentence to a man's reputation if her infidelity results in children whom she passes off as his. This happened with my own parents. My father's political enemies used the marital difficulties my parents had after my older brother was born to cast doubt on my younger sister Layla's and my paternity."

Sebastian whistled. "Well, I investigated that jerk, and found that he was sent by one Nedal Aal Ajam, renowned political enemy of the Aal Ferjanis, denouncer of the King and number one beneficiary if ever the royal family of Khumayrah was overthrown."

"*Aih, hadda suheeh.* That's true. He would have latched onto any public discord between Sabrina and me to plant doubt about the authenticity of our marriage. Just like in my mother's case, who was herself only half Khumayran, they would have played on the fact that Sabrina is a foreigner.

In my mother's case, they said that she sought revenge as well as emotional and sexual freedom outside the restrictions of the loveless union. The lie that Layla and I were not the King's offspring chased us through half of our lives, until my father was forced to refute the allegations with medical evidence. Of course, his wrath was severe. Anyone who'd help spread the rumors paid dearly for their transgressions."

"I can imagine. To force a king, from a culture as big on macho pride as yours, to defend his wife's honor and his children's legitimacy—that's huge. But the example he'd made of those who'd defamed you hasn't deterred others from trying the same trick?"

"The potential gains are great enough to risk consequences. And they don't need to go as far as the others went. If they can prove any of the royal wives unsatisfied, they won't need to cast doubts over the legitimacy of the union's offspring. It's enough to start a campaign of ridicule that a man who can't govern and fulfill his own wife isn't fit to govern a nation or fulfill its needs. Our political situation is complex enough at the moment that a battle on this front might tip the balance in our enemies' favor."

"But you have nothing to worry about," Sebastian assured. "Whatever those backstabbers are trying to do, after last night, there's no way anyone could say that Sabrina is unsatisfied. The woman is clearly crazy in love with you. The whole world now has photographic evidence of that fact."

There was another moment of silence. Then Adham exhaled heavily. "I guess they do."

Sabrina turned around, stumbled away.

She somehow found herself back in her car, agony clamping each muscle, her heart flapping in her chest like a wounded bird. She dropped her head to the steering wheel.

It was far uglier than the worst thing she'd believed before.

She'd believed he'd seduced her for the land and a necessary heir. She'd thought he'd only put on a show in public, as Sebastian had so astutely realized, as a preventive measure against wagging tongues and social nuisance.

Then last night she'd come to believe he'd always been attracted to her but her father's deal had hardened his heart, making him treat their marriage as nothing but a business deal. She'd believed he'd lost control when she'd pulled away in public, acting spontaneously for the first time, baring his real desires, which he'd hidden from even himself.

She'd been a fool. He hadn't lost control. His actions had been *damage* control. Which he had to perform indefinitely. As long as his enemies watched him.

Her public rejection had been what he'd been guarding against all along, as it would have destroyed his projection of a blissful marriage that was vital to his image, to the stability of his ruling house.

So he'd seduced her again, to make her fall in with his plans. *Again.*

And if she hadn't been so desperate to be with him again, she would have remained in his bed, unaware of the truth. She would have continued putting on the show he needed, fooling his enemies with the sincerity of her ardor.

And being made a fool of for the rest of her life.

Adham had left Sebastian an hour ago.

He'd been driving aimlessly ever since. For the first time in his life, he felt at a loss.

He needed some time to come to terms with what had happened last night. It had been more than explosive sex. It had been nothing like the first time he'd taken her.

This time, when he'd made her his, she'd made him hers.

His father had said this would be his fate, just as it had been his own—to find one irreplaceable woman where he least expected, to want her with everything in him, to love her till the end of his days.

But did she love him?

He'd felt his heart clench as if on a burning coal when Sebastian announced that she did, as a forgone conclusion.

For he truly didn't know.

He had no doubt she wanted him with every fiber of her voluptuous body. But what about her heart?

There were too many considerations that made him fear her heart wasn't involved. Or worse, couldn't and wouldn't be.

She had been at her lowest moments when she'd fallen into his arms. She had needed his support, in more ways than one. Now, she might still be reeling from her father's loss, needing to cling to him to fill the void of security. What if her feelings for him were gratitude and need mixed with lust? The gratitude he could do without, the need he accepted as her right as his wife, the lust he craved. But none of this constituted love. And he couldn't live knowing she didn't love him as wholeheartedly as he loved her.

There was one way to discover the truth. A test.

He dreaded the result. He didn't know if he could live with it if he learned that she didn't and could never love him. But he had to do it.

He couldn't live not knowing for certain, either.

Hours later, he returned home, and felt it immediately.

A psychic vacuum. An absence.

He tore through the house looking for her. But even as he dashed from one place to another, calling out her name, he knew.

She was gone.

On his third time storming to his bedroom, which had been theirs for only one night, he saw something he hadn't noticed before on his bedside table.

A note.

He approached it as if it were a live grenade, unfolding it with the care of someone defusing a bomb.

But there was no defusing the destruction in the note.

Only four words. *I want a divorce.*

Nine

After the disbelief and devastation, Adham called Sabrina's cell phone for thirty minutes straight.

Each time the phone rang until it disconnected.

He careened through the house, raising hell, interrogating everyone within sight, not caring that he was revealing to his subordinates that he had no idea where his wife was.

He was at his wit's end when the bodyguards he'd asked to keep an eye on her, and whom he'd forgotten about in his madness, called. They'd said she'd gone back home. Her family home.

The two hours it took him to get to Grant Vineyards and Winery taught him the meaning of agony.

By the time he spotted her, a bright white figure in the distance among the verdant vines, he felt he'd aged two decades.

He strode after her receding figure through the uniform rows of vines that seemed to stretch into infinity, adding to his impression that he'd never reach her. So much crowded inside him—anger, dread, heartache—he felt he'd explode with it all.

It felt like the distance between them widened instead of narrowed with each step. It was too much.

He bellowed with it. *"Sabrina!"*

His shout seemed to freeze her and everything else, as if all existence had been paused. He felt as if his feet barely touched ground as he closed the distance separating them.

He came to an abrupt halt a foot away, vibrating with emotion. Her scent flayed him. He could discern every hair in the gleaming mahogany waves that cascaded down her back, feel each tremor her heart sent through her flesh. And he knew.

He was damned to love her, even without hope of reciprocation. What she evoked in him was the only thing he would ever want or need. And she didn't feel the same.

He could do nothing but accept it, and take whatever he could from her.

Feeling defeated for the first time in his life, he declared his surrender.

"So now you realize your power over me," he rasped. "You're raising the stakes. Go ahead, Sabrina. If you want to make a new deal with new terms, then make it."

She turned to him then, her face and voice inanimate. "I want one thing. To never see you again."

He advanced on her. She tried to retreat. He wouldn't let her, grabbing her arm, shoving the dossier he'd brought at her.

Her fingers closed around it instinctively, her eyes blank, making him feel as if she didn't even see him.

But he had to try to make her see, try to make her

respond to him. "I thought this would show me if you felt anything real for me, but it's no longer a test. I can no longer afford it. You can consider all of this an incentive. And you can ask for anything at all in addition. Just stay with me, give us a chance. I know we started badly, but we can make this work. I know we can."

She wrenched away as if his hand burned her. "This act will never work."

So she'd been acting all the time?

The thought swamped him with a despondence so profound, it made him realize one thing. The most important thing.

Even if he found the right price to make her stay, it would kill him knowing she felt nothing for him.

He had to let her go, no matter the damages to himself, his heart, or his kingdom. No matter if she were already pregnant with his child. He'd rather be exiled from his homeland than live knowing he had her in every way but was forever exiled from her heart.

Unable to face her or bear the agony, he turned away.

"What *is* this?"

Her exclamation hit him between the shoulder blades, making him turn against his will, against his better judgment.

He found her flipping through the dossier, her frown deepening. The shuffling sounds chafed his nerves, snapping them one by one. He waited with thorns in his heart for delight to invade her eyes, once she realized all she wanted was hers for the taking, with nothing required on her part.

But it wasn't delight that filled her eyes. It was rage.

His confusion turned to stupefaction as she threw the dossier to the ground and proceeded to shred the contracts and deeds for everything he'd promised her once she fulfilled her part of the deal.

"See this, Adham?" she shouted. "This is what I think of the deal you and my father made! You can take your land and assets and terms and shove them! You think I want to inherit my father's land and business? I want them *gone*. I want them to have never existed. They've been the cause of all the alienation I've felt my whole life. Everyone who's ever come within five feet of me had their eyes on them, including you. So if *you* no longer want the land, you can give it to charity or let the wild reclaim it for all I care.

"*I* never wanted any of this. The only thing I ever wanted from my father was love, the only thing I wanted to do was help him. I chose my fields of study so I'd be the right hand he'd always implied a *son* would have been. I'm good for more than being married off and making babies like he—and you—thought. I certainly don't need either of you to 'provide' for me. I am a professional any winemaking business in the world would hire in a flash at the salary I demand."

Adham could only gape at her as she continued her furious tirade.

"As for you, the only thing I ever wanted from you was caring and respect. But those are alien concepts to you and the only thing I now *need* from you is an uncontested divorce!"

With each word from her trembling lips, realization and heart-bursting delight dawned on Adham.

She'd never wanted the things he'd thought she'd married him for. She hadn't been in on her father's deal, and had always thought their marriage was real.

She'd *wanted* to marry him. Because she wanted him. Because she loved him!

So why did she want to leave him now?

"*Arjooki, ya habibati,* I don't understand. I love you—"

"Stop it!" she screamed. "Stop acting. I heard you, Adham. Today, with Sebastian. Your only concern is to allay doubts about our marriage so your enemies won't undermine your family's power. I understand it's a noble cause but count me out. Go acquire some other woman to do this job. I want—I *deserve* someone who doesn't have to pretend to want me."

And everything fell into place.

He surged toward her. "*Habibati,* I beg you, listen to me—"

She beat his hands away. "Oh, I did. I've done nothing but listen to you and your lies since the day I met you. But I've listened to the truth today, and nothing you say can change that."

He still vibrated with the elation of discovering her reciprocated emotions. But now, as her anguish flayed him, anxiety rose to supplant it as the extent of her misapprehension registered. He rushed to explain.

"But you misunderstood. I was discussing with Sebastian my predicament in retrospect, answering his questions about what my enemies had hoped to gain by approaching him."

"Oh, please. Last night was about bringing me back under your spell, to be your worshipping fool and provide your enemies with photographic evidence of my enslavement. You must have also deemed it necessary to sleep with me again, to get working on the heir you need."

His aching hands clenched on the need to drag her against him, make her listen to him, make her believe him. His heart stampeded with the rising dread that she might not, might close her heart to him, that he'd done it too much damage to fix. But he couldn't accept that, never would. He'd make her believe him.

"No, Sabrina, that isn't how—"

She cut him off. "That is exactly how it was. But don't worry. There won't be any repercussions from divorcing me. You were lucky—the two times you slept with me happened to be at the exact wrong time."

"I don't care if you never get pregnant," he protested.

"Save it, Adham. And look at it this way. Our divorce will bring in even more business for the club. More people will be rabidly curious to see you next season with a new acquisition."

He stared at her. Sabrina as he'd never seen her. A spirit that needed nothing and no one, that could not be tamed or bought, but would give her all willingly, endlessly only in the name of love. A tigress capable of slashing anyone who trespassed against her to shreds.

He knew he was fighting for his life here—for she was his life—but he couldn't control the thrill that took him over at discovering these new facets of her. The knowledge of the barbed steel beneath the silk and surrender would make him revel in them more. He couldn't wait to unearth more complexities, which he was now certain she possessed. But none of that would happen, his very life would be over, if he didn't convince her of his sincerity. As he must.

Ready now to take her bitterness, welcoming its pain in atonement for the pain he'd caused her, determined to wipe it away, he closed the distance she'd put between them.

"It was Sebastian who said what happened between us last night was good for business. But he was only right about one thing—I had nothing on my mind but you. I'd come to claim you, thinking that if desire was all you felt for me, that I was a fool not to let you have me. But you turned away and I lost all sense of place and purpose. All sense, period. I had to get you back, make you succumb to the hunger that was eating at both of us."

She shook her head, wrenched away. He caught her back, persisted. "But after last night, I was in agony. I didn't know if you were just taking whatever benefits you could from our situation while your heart remained untouched. I went back to our house to give you what I just gave you now, what you tore apart, what would have released you from any fear about your future. I thought if you chose to stay with me when you no longer had to, that it would mean you do want me beyond what I can provide.

"But you have given me more than I ever dreamed. As you have from day one. It was so good, so unbelievable between us from the start, that when your father approached me with his offer, I found it easier to believe that none of it had been true, that *you'd* been too good to be true. But you are my miracle. And the fact that you love me, after all your father and I did, is beyond a miracle."

Her tear-filled eyes hardened.

His heart sank. "You don't still love me?"

"You are still acting. You just need a baby to tick off some royal requirement and don't want to go through the trouble of acquiring another wife. It was a very time-consuming enterprise for you, acquiring me. All those times you pretended to be interested in me must have been torture for you. A word of advice. Next time, forgo the pretense and just lay your terms on the table. I'm sure hordes of suitable women will snap up you and your cold-blooded deal in a second."

"I only ever wanted you. The only pretense was when I pretended I didn't." He stopped as more tears escaped her eyes, groaned. "But I can't ask you to believe me. Words mean nothing. I have to prove the truth of my feelings with actions."

He got out his cell phone and dialed a number.

He spoke as soon as the line opened. "Angus Henderson? Sheikh Adham Aal Ferjani. I have a scoop for you. Record what I'm going to say so you have it in my own words. Are you ready?" He waited a second, gazing back at Sabrina's confused, apprehensive stare. Then he started. "This is Sheikh Adham Aal Ferjani of Khumayrah, and I'm here today to divulge the true circumstances of my marriage...."

Sabrina gaped at Adham as he recounted everything from the start. He painted his actions in their worst light, closing by saying he was fighting to convince his wife, the love of his life, to give him a second chance to atone for his sins against her, so he could prove his love and dedicate his life to her.

Then he ended the call. "Do you understand now I care only that you believe me and remain my wife, lover and soul mate?"

Sabrina could only stare at him in shock. Angus Henderson was one of the country's most famous celebrity reporters, who produced and hosted the most notorious shows in the history of modern media. And Adham had just told him everything about their marriage. Everything.

That Adham would expose himself like that! That he would think nothing of offering himself to the media to eat him alive as long as it proved his sincerity to her.

Her paralysis suddenly snapped, and she snatched Adham's phone, redialed the reporter's number. Angus answered at once. No doubt the reporter was rabidly eager to answer in case Adham had forgotten more juicy details to add to the explosive scoop he'd just secured.

"Mr. Henderson? This is Sabrina Grant—Princess Aal Ferjani—Mrs. Adham Aal Ferjan..." She panted, her words and thoughts tangling. "Oh, you know who I am. Everything Adham told you was a joke. A dare. There is *no* truth in what he said, so please don't publish anything."

There was a moment's silence on the other end, before the man's signature raspy voice answered, "I'm sorry to hear that, since I just broadcast his recording live. In fact, you, too, are on the air with me right now."

"Oh, God, no...."

She felt she'd burn to ashes with mortification. Adham took the phone from her, assuring their live audience that he'd meant every word and wouldn't be issuing a retraction. Sabrina squirmed, protesting, but Adham only smiled down on her, hugging her to him as he terminated the call.

"Do you believe me now, *ya rohi?*"

She tore out of his arms and stumbled back. "Believe you? You painted yourself blacker than I ever had! What will that mean for you in your kingdom? I can only assume the worst. You big fool!" Then she threw her arms around him and smothered him in kisses. Tears flowed faster as his mingled with hers. He'd just proved he was as far gone in love with her as she was with him, and feared losing her as much. "Oh, *ya habibi,*" she sobbed, "I might have been reluctant to believe you right away, but I would have eventually. You didn't have to go to this extreme."

He shook his head. "I did. I couldn't let you doubt my love for you a moment longer. I couldn't risk that you'd always feel some distrust. I had to *agt'a ash'shak bel yaqeen*—cleave doubt with certainty, once and forever."

"You don't have to," she insisted. "I will never doubt you again. Please, tell that man to announce a retraction."

"I won't. It's my punishment for letting myself be blinded to the truth, your truth. It's my thanks to you for saving me from spending my life without you, and in misery."

"If you want to thank me, you won't punish yourself.

I can't bear seeing you suffer in any way. And what will your family, your father, think?"

"I couldn't care less. I'll take care of any fallout. The only thing that matters to me is what you think and feel, and that you give me the chance to prove my love to you."

A fresh stream of tears, of delight and gratitude, poured down her cheeks. "More than this?"

He pressed her against his body that trembled with emotion. "I haven't even started. I intend to do everything in my power, everything I can think of. And believe me, I can think of endless ways to prove my love."

"I promise you the same." She looked up at him, felt her heart quivering with adoration for this magnificent man, *her* man, for real, forever, even as a mischievous grin played on her lips. "Wanna bet I'll think of more things than you can?"

"Hmm, sounds like we've got a challenge on our hands. I like that. You know me and challenges—I never lose."

She melted back into his arms, sighing her bliss. "And I might just let you win...."

* * * * *

Don't miss the final anthology in
A SUMMER FOR SCANDAL
WINNING IT ALL
Featuring stories from USA TODAY *bestselling author*
Catherine Mann and Emily McKay
Available August 10, 2010
From Silhouette Desire

COMING NEXT MONTH

Available August 10, 2010

#2029 HONOR-BOUND GROOM
Yvonne Lindsay
Man of the Month

#2030 FALLING FOR HIS PROPER MISTRESS
Tessa Radley
Dynasties: The Jarrods

#2031 WINNING IT ALL
"Pregnant with the Playboy's Baby"—Catherine Mann
"His Accidental Fiancée"—Emily McKay
A Summer for Scandal

#2032 EXPECTANT PRINCESS, UNEXPECTED AFFAIR
Michelle Celmer
Royal Seductions

#2033 THE BILLIONAIRE'S BABY ARRANGEMENT
Charlene Sands
Napa Valley Vows

#2034 HIS BLACK SHEEP BRIDE
Anna DePalo

REQUEST YOUR FREE BOOKS!

2 FREE NOVELS
PLUS 2
FREE GIFTS!

Passionate, Powerful, Provocative!

YES! Please send me 2 FREE Silhouette Desire® novels and my 2 FREE gifts (gifts are worth about $10). After receiving them, if I don't wish to receive any more books, I can return the shipping statement marked "cancel." If I don't cancel, I will receive 6 brand-new novels every month and be billed just $4.05 per book in the U.S. or $4.74 per book in Canada. That's a saving of at least 15% off the cover price! It's quite a bargain! Shipping and handling is just 50¢ per book.* I understand that accepting the 2 free books and gifts places me under no obligation to buy anything. I can always return a shipment and cancel at any time. Even if I never buy another book, the two free books and gifts are mine to keep forever.

225/326 SDN E5QG

Name	(PLEASE PRINT)	
Address		Apt. #
City	State/Prov.	Zip/Postal Code

Signature (if under 18, a parent or guardian must sign)

Mail to the Silhouette Reader Service:
IN U.S.A.: P.O. Box 1867, Buffalo, NY 14240-1867
IN CANADA: P.O. Box 609, Fort Erie, Ontario L2A 5X3

Not valid for current subscribers to Silhouette Desire books.

Want to try two free books from another line?
Call 1-800-873-8635 or visit www.morefreebooks.com.

* Terms and prices subject to change without notice. Prices do not include applicable taxes. N.Y. residents add applicable sales tax. Canadian residents will be charged applicable provincial taxes and GST. Offer not valid in Quebec. This offer is limited to one order per household. All orders subject to approval. Credit or debit balances in a customer's account(s) may be offset by any other outstanding balance owed by or to the customer. Please allow 4 to 6 weeks for delivery. Offer available while quantities last.

Your Privacy: Silhouette Books is committed to protecting your privacy. Our Privacy Policy is available online at www.eHarlequin.com or upon request from the Reader Service. From time to time we make our lists of customers available to reputable third parties who may have a product or service of interest to you. If you would prefer we not share your name and address, please check here. ☐

Help us get it right—We strive for accurate, respectful and relevant communications. To clarify or modify your communication preferences, visit us at www.ReaderService.com/consumerschoice.

SDES10R

Five hunky Texas single fathers—five stories from
Cathy Gillen Thacker's LONE STAR DADS *miniseries.*
Here's an excerpt from the latest, THE MOMMY PROPOSAL
from Harlequin American Romance.

"I hear you work miracles," Nate Hutchinson drawled.
Brooke Mitchell had just stepped into his lavishly appointed
office in downtown Fort Worth, Texas.

"Sometimes, I do." Brooke smiled and took the sexy
financier's hand in hers, shook it briefly.

"Good." Nate looked her straight in the eye. "Because
I'm in need of a home makeover—fast. The son of an old
friend is coming to live with me."

She was still tingling from the feel of his warm palm.
"Temporarily or permanently?"

"If all goes according to plan, I'll adopt Landry by
summer's end."

Brooke had heard the founder of Nate Hutchinson
Financial Services was eligible, wealthy and generous to a
fault. She hadn't known he was in the market for a family,
but she supposed she shouldn't be surprised. But Brooke
had figured a man as successful and handsome as Nate
would want one the old-fashioned way. *Not that this was
any of her business...*

"So what's the child like?" she asked crisply, trying not
to think how the marine-blue of Nate's dress shirt deepened
the hue of his eyes.

"I don't know." Nate took a seat behind his massive
antique mahogany desk. He relaxed against the smooth
leather of the chair. "I've never met him."

"Yet you've invited this kid to live with you permanently?"

"It's complicated. But I'm sure it's going to be fine."

Obviously Nate Hutchinson knew as little about teenage

boys as he did about decorating. But that wasn't her problem. Finding a way to do the assignment without getting the least bit emotionally involved was.

Find out how a young boy brings Nate and Brooke
together in THE MOMMY PROPOSAL,
coming August 2010 from Harlequin American Romance.

HARLEQUIN® Blaze™

THE HEAT IS ON
by
Jill Shalvis

The attraction between Bella and
Detective Madden is undeniable.
But can a few wild encounters
turn into love?

Don't miss this hot read.

*Available in August
where books are sold.*

___

red-hot reads

www.eHarlequin.com